# HARMONY *and* HEARTBREAK

## A SUITEHEARTS NOVEL

# SUITE HEARTS

1

# HARMONY
## - and -
# HEARTBREAK

## CLAIRE KANN

**HARPER**

*An Imprint of HarperCollinsPublishers*

Library of Congress Control Number: 2022943677
ISBN 978-0-06-306939-8
Typography by Chris Kwon
22 23 24 25 26  LBC  5 4 3 2 1

First Edition

For Cinni—my very first Matchmaker

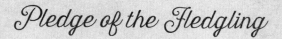

# Pledge of the Fledgling

From now until I ascend, I promise to
follow my Kindlings' hearts, create fun
and inventive Singes, listen to my matchmaking
elders, always be true to my talent, learn from
my experiences, challenge myself to magnificence,
operate with honesty and integrity, meet
the expectations of the Matchmaker Oracle
Council, and if I must fail,
I will do so with honor and grace.

This is my vow as a Fledgling Matchmaker.

# Chapter 1

From now until I ascend,
I promise to create fun and inventive Singes.

L iving in Hotel Coeur's penthouse suite impressed
*everyone.*

Rose's friends all assumed she was an heiress. One
year, rumors about her family being royalty in hiding
had even spread like wildfire through her school. In reality, they were just your run-of-the-mill, average magical
Matchmakers—humans with the ability to inspire love in
the hearts of strangers—doing their best to get by.

Well. Sort of.

There was nothing *average* about Rose Seville.

Twirling down the third-floor hallway with headphones
in her ears, she sang wholeheartedly—and tragically—
off-key. She imagined herself as a hopeful wannabe pop
star on a reality TV audition. One shot to make it big. One
shot to reach her dreams. A shimmy, one-two step, and a

failed whistle note later, she knocked on the door for room 306 three times.

No one answered.

Undeterred, Rose hit pause on her music and knocked again . . . and kept knocking harder and faster without stopping until the door suddenly flew open. "Good morning!" she chirped brightly, giving him her best customer-service smile.

A bleary-eyed man in wrinkled plain pajamas squinted back at her. His name was Daniel Eugene Shideler, and Rose was about to change his entire life. He was one of her Kindlings—the person she'd been assigned to help.

"Can I help you with something?" he asked in a low, gruffy voice.

*Ooh.* Promising.

The best shortcut to judging someone's character? Wake them up unexpectedly. Usually when Rose pulled her rise-and-shine stunt, guests screamed and slammed doors and complained to the front desk.

"You can!" she said with extra cheer. "Thank you so much for asking. I'm Rose. My family owns this hotel."

He dragged a hand down his face. "Okay? So?"

"Sooooo, this is for you." Rose held out the charmed coupon for him to take. "One free pastry and drink of your choice from the Courtyard Cart, courtesy of Hotel Coeur. It's good until nine a.m. today."

"But it's, like, eight thirty now."

Rose grinned. The corners of her mouth curled up toward her cheeks as if she were the Grinch about to steal Christmas. "Guess you better hurry, then."

As soon as Daniel's fingers touched the coupon, the familiar tingle of Rose's powers working rippled across her skin, an eruption of cool and exhilarating goose bumps. Her eyes flashed, turning purple—her personal Matchmaker color—before fading to her normal brown.

"Great. Enjoy your stay," she said, wiggling her fingers at him in goodbye.

Matchmaker magic was limited by lots of strict rules. They couldn't make someone lovesick or fall in love. Mind reading was absolutely, 100 percent forbidden. And they had to respect free will—people could choose to ignore a Matchmaker's magical influence if they truly wanted to.

Rose had placed a temptation charm on the coupon that would make Daniel, a self-described doughnut fiend, have an instantaneous craving for a good Boston cream. She knew in her heart she'd see him downstairs before 9:00 a.m. Music back on, she strutted toward the elevators.

Hotel Coeur had been in the Seville family for five generations and had three elevators. Rose preferred the middle carriage. Did they all look the same—golden doors with gold-rimmed mirrors and marble floors? Yes. They didn't *feel* the same though. She couldn't put her finger on why, other than it felt "alive." Which was just creepy enough that she never told anyone about it.

Everything in Hotel Coeur was renovated regularly, stayed up to code, and had on-site maintenance twenty-four hours a day, but something about this elevator stood out. It had personality like an old tree in the woods. It had seen things, enduring them all in silence and storing them within its long, long memory. And it felt almost ready to spill its secrets, pulsing with anticipation as it waited for the perfect moment. Rose hoped to be there when it happened.

After a short ride down to the lobby, Rose danced her way to the courtyard, lip-syncing in silence so she didn't disturb normal business operations—the bustling café bursting with patrons, the employees at the front desk checking in a large group for a family reunion, the people waiting for taxis or working while sitting in the too-comfy armchairs and sofas strategically placed around the edges of the room. She continued toward the back of the lobby and straight through a pair of double doors leading outside.

If Hotel Coeur had a heart, it'd be the massive weeping willow tree at the center of the courtyard. Its long, deep-green leaves reached toward the ground, swaying gently in the soft morning breeze, and a rock garden with a bed of hydrangeas flourished at the base of the tree. Several round white tables for two and off-pink benches fanned out around it as well.

Rose's cousin, Cora, was waiting for her there. Hair split down the middle and styled into two long braids, she had a warm brown skin tone and wore a black dress and white tennis shoes with rainbow shoelaces. She looked anxious and kind of twitchy—impending Singes always made her nervous for some reason. As if they had anything to worry about.

"Did he take it?" Cora asked immediately.

"*Of course* he did," Rose said.

Cora chewed on her bottom lip. "Maggie is still in position."

"*Of course* she is."

Daniel and Margaret Renee Krauss (who insisted on being called Maggie) had been assigned to be Rose's Kindlings exactly two days and fifteen hours ago. If Rose completed this Singe within the next twenty minutes, it would be the fastest one she's ever completed—a new personal best.

Rose reached out, grabbing Cora's hand. "Our plan is brilliant. Stop worrying so much."

There were five foolproof steps to set up a Singe—the spark of connection between Kindlings, which created the *possibility* for love between people who needed the connection most.

Step one: connection—establishing the psychic bond linking a Matchmaker and their Kindling together, making them feel like fast friends in a getaway car speeding away toward forever. It also made a Kindling more pliable to Matchmaker influence, which helped with . . .

Step two: Kindling's heart—discovering their Kindling's true desire and gaining access to their heartstrings. Heartstrings were exactly what they sounded like. Technically, they were a physical manifestation of the desires that could be found only in one's heart, and they happened to look like strings.

Rose wanted to challenge herself, choosing to only bond with Maggie (with her parents' approval, of course). Once a Matchmaker knew what kind of love their Kindling's heart desired, they could then begin setting up the appropriate Singe. Maggie's heart had been broken more times than Rose could count. She was never afraid to put herself out there, and so far, getting crushed hadn't stopped her from wanting to try again. Her Mr. Right was out there—she felt it in her soul and believed in it a little bit more with every passing day. Rose figured all Maggie needed was an opportunity. Right place, right time. She'd see Daniel, and her heart would immediately take over.

Next up was step three: compatibility—using all the information they've collected about their Kindlings to create the perfect stage for a perfect Singe.

Trying it one-sided, relying only on Maggie with some

help from Daniel's public social media profiles, turned out to be easier than Rose thought.

They were both from Omaha, Nebraska, of all places, and loved reading high-fantasy novels and watching black-and-white movies. Maggie had recently graduated from college after studying architecture. Meanwhile Daniel never went, instead pursuing his dream of becoming a pilot (source: a photo of him holding his newly minted license and long text post with way too much personal information, if you asked Cora).

And strangely, they both loved Boston cream dough-nuts.

Thus, the *doughnut pass me by* meet-cute was born.

Rose rubbed her hands together. "Let's get rid of Samantha before Daniel gets here."

Cora nodded, following her lead as they walked over to the small food cart with a giant lavender umbrella. It served a rotating menu depending on the time of day. In the morning, they sold only pastries, doughnuts, fruit, cereal bars, and drinks.

Samantha had pulled her frizzy copper-colored hair into the café-employee-required bun. Several wayward curls had escaped, framing her face. The freckles that dusted her upturned nose were the same color as her big brown eyes, which perfectly complemented her dusky skin tone. When she saw them coming, she smiled at Cora before frowning at Rose, who glared back.

Why wasn't it illegal for someone to be so pretty and so *mean* at the same time? "It's time for your break," Rose said to her. She pointed to her parents, who sat at the table nestled in the southeast corner of the courtyard, the perfect spot for them to supervise her Singe attempt. "They asked me to fill in until you get back."

"Sure, brat."

Divine intervention must have stopped Rose from rolling her eyes because she sure was about to.

"No, really," Cora chimed in. "I'm supposed to watch her."

"Oh, okay. I believe *you*," Samantha said, beginning to take off her apron. She handed it to Cora. "In that case, back in thirty."

Rose pouted. As soon as Samantha was out of earshot, she said, "I really don't like her."

"Pretty sure that feeling is mutual."

"You're not helping."

Cora laughed. "Well, I never agreed to do that."

"Ooh, here he comes," Rose said.

Daniel's stringy brown hair stood straight up on all sides. Rose tried not to laugh, but he totally looked like that picture of Albert Einstein from her science textbook. Temptation charms were so basic, Matchmaker babies could do it. Charms and enchantments really didn't force people to do anything—they just gave the person a tiny push in the direction they were already headed. He *wanted* to be there, just like Rose thought.

Once he reached the cart, he said, "You again."

Rose grinned her Grinchiest grin.

Daniel asked, "Why am I not surprised to see you here?"

"I don't know. Must be destiny." She shrugged playfully, and Cora poked her in the side. "What can I get you?"

Daniel glanced at the cart's menu, rubbing the side of his neck while he decided. "You wouldn't happen to have any Boston creams, would you?"

"Um." Rose pretended to check the cart's inventory under the counter. "We might in the kitchen, if you don't mind waiting a few minutes."

"I'll get it," Cora volunteered, and dashed away.

Right as Cora went inside, Maggie entered the courtyard. Her sleek dark hair was the flawless contrast to Daniel's. It had a shine like raven feathers in the sun and framed her heart-shaped face. Every morning since she checked in, she ordered a cup of coffee at exactly 9:05 a.m. and sat in the courtyard for an hour to work.

"Rose, good morning," Maggie said. "Didn't expect to see you here."

"I'm filling in for someone while they're on break."

Maggie frowned. "Is that legal? Are they paying you?"

Rose shook her head. "But I'm going to inherit the hotel someday, so it balances out."

"I suppose," Maggie said, pulling her wallet out of her purse. "I'll have a coffee. And are there any more of those?"

Cora, blessed with perfect punctual timing, appeared at Rose's side holding one, count it: one, delectable doughnut in a plastic container for Daniel. "Oh, sorry," she said, passing the Conduit to him. "This is the last one."

Step four: create a Conduit—a bespelled item used to facilitate a connection between Kindlings. It acted as a magical primer, opening their hearts to accept the power of a Singe.

Daniel took one look at Maggie while holding the doughnut and said, "*Oh.* Um. Y-You can have it."

"Oh, I couldn't!" Maggie said.

"No, really I insist. I, um, you, uh—" He laughed, completely flustered.

"We could share it?" Maggie suggested. "Are you busy? I usually grab a table and work for a little while."

"I would love to," he said as they walked off.

Step five: Singe—and Rose's Kindlings were off to the races. She smiled watching them go. The second they shared a bite of their Conduit doughnut the Singe would be complete.

"Don't forget these!" Rose quickly handed Daniel two

forks, both infused with a *Candy Girl* charm to make them desire something sweet to eat. Just to be safe.

Across the courtyard, her dad gave her two thumbs up.

Magical Matchmaker mission accomplished.

## Chapter 2

From now until I ascend,
I promise to challenge myself to magnificence.

The next day while blissfully asleep, Cora jolted awake when something cold pressed against her legs. She turned over, shouting, *"Why do you always do that?"*

Rose buried her face in one of Cora's many, many pillows, shoulders shaking with muffled laughter. And then she pushed her frosty feet against her cousin's legs again.

"CUT IT OUT!" Cora threw a pillow at her.

"Then wake up!"

"No, it's too early."

Cora had never and would never be a morning person. Sleeping ranked top two on her list of favorite things to do, and it wasn't number two. There was something otherworldly, magical, incredible, ethereal about diving into a tidy bed with soft sheets, an abundance of pillows, and a comforter stuffed with the softest feathers on earth.

Her parents usually let her sleep in as long as she wanted, even if that meant she had only five minutes to get ready for school. Eventually, they figured, it would teach her a lesson. Unfortunately, they severely underestimated her love of sleep.

Double unfortunately, those days were long gone.

"We're gonna be late for school if you don't get up," Rose said.

"Too. Early," Cora said. "And since *when* do you care about school?"

"I don't, but you do." Rose laughed. "My mom said she's making pancakes for us."

"I'm not getting up yet." Cora burrowed back under the blankets, snuggling down. "Good day. Get out."

"Mmm, yeah you are. Get up!"

"I said, GOOD DAY."

Rose whined, "Come on, get up, get up, get up, get up." She threw herself across Cora, wrapping her arms and legs around her. "Up, up, up, up!"

"Get off meeeeeeee!" Cora squeezed her eyes shut and pulled her blanket up to her chin. She'd been dreaming about a place with endless green grass fields and a beautiful cornflower-blue sky. A familiar voice kept calling her name through the blustery wind. No matter how hard she searched, she couldn't find them anywhere. Sometimes, if too much time didn't pass, she could go back to her dream and pick up where she left off.

"It's not just pancakes. My mom said she has something important to tell us."

Cora peered at her cousin with one eye. "What is it?"

"I don't know, and we won't know unless you get up. It's a surprise."

"I don't like surprises," Cora grumbled. The last surprise that got thrown at her involved her parents moving to Europe without her because the Matchmaker Oracle Council needed them for a special project.

Her parents were Career Matchmakers—meaning they worked directly for the Oracle Council, investigating and providing support for Singes gone wrong all over the world. Last Friday, they told her that they'd just landed in Rome. One of the cases there involved three Matchmakers, four Kindlings, and two identical Conduits that got mixed up. Her mom said it was a *complete* mess.

Wherever the Oracle Council sent them, they had to go. Cora had been allowed to join them a few times before, but this special project would be too long. They said she needed to go to school, have a normal life—well, normal for a Matchmaker. So, six months ago they shipped her off to San Francisco to live with her aunt and uncle in Hotel Coeur.

Basically, ruining her *entire* life.

"I'm sure it'll be fine. She seemed excited about it, so it must be good."

Cora yawned and sat up, pushing Rose to the side as she did. Reluctantly, she got out of bed to go get dressed. She trudged into the kitchen nearly thirty minutes later, wearing her school uniform and fuzzy bunny house slippers.

Rose was already sitting at the bar, and her mom, Tanya, was plating food by the stove. Her dad, Norman, stood on the other side of the counter with his arms crossed. Tall and wide with biceps bigger than her head, no one ever suspected he was a kindhearted Matchmaker—one of the best in their region. His bald head, dark brown skin, bushy eyebrows, and the fact that he exuded pure security guard energy probably didn't help that image any.

And every time Cora saw him, her chest instantly got tight.

Twins like her dad and her uncle were so rare among Matchmakers they literally made news when they were born because Matchmakers usually didn't have siblings. No one knew why—or at least that's what everyone claimed.

Sometimes, Cora walked into a room, spotted him, and it was like her brain got confused. She saw her uncle and thought, *Dad. My dad is back.* Her heart skipped a surprised beat, her feet wanted to run, and she got so happy it took her breath away. But then his features really began to register. . . .

Her dad absolutely *hated* being bald.

It wasn't him. It was never him.

And then, she got so sad, so fast it felt like she was being crushed under an avalanche of snow.

"Good morning," Cora said glumly as she took a seat next to Rose.

Aunt Tanya set down full plates of pancakes and bacon and gave them each a mug of hot chocolate. Cora was immediately suspicious. This breakfast felt like a bribe. *Oh, we have bad news, so have something delicious to wash it all down!* She said thank you, anyway.

Rose wasted no time drowning her pancakes in syrup and taking a huge bite. She asked, "So what's up?" with her mouth full.

"Well," Aunt Tanya said, "last night the Oracle Council sent us a message. They've been very impressed with your performance lately and have decided to accelerate your training."

"What does that mean?" Cora asked, and thought, *They can't possibly be impressed with* me. It made sense for Rose since the Oracle Council had co-named her best in their generation, the Wunderkind, with Julien Swift. But Cora was . . . not. Sometimes she thought less of herself when she stood next to Rose.

"It means they've decided to allow you to take your Flyer exam early."

"Early?!" Rose jumped out of her chair in excitement, while Cora shrank down into hers, shoulders near her ears.

Young Matchmakers-in-training were called Fledglings. Right now, they had to check in daily with their research progress, their plans had to be approved before being put into action, and they were, under no circumstances, allowed to perform a Singe unsupervised. Sometime after their thirteenth birthday, they would take their final exam to become Flyers. It was sort of like going from having a learner's permit to a driver's license. More independence but also way more responsibilities.

Uncle Norman said, "*If* you're able to successfully complete two challenge Singes on your own, then yes, you will be allowed to take your Flyer exam early. It's an extremely rare and special opportunity. The Oracle Council only does this once in a blue moon."

"How early are we talking here?" Rose persisted.

"Shortly after finishing your challenges," Aunt Tanya said. "The first will be a solo Singe assignment designed to challenge your greatest weakness or fear as a Matchmaker. Because it's a test, guardians can only intervene if it's an emergency, and even then, that could still count against your overall score."

"I'm going to fail, then," Cora muttered. She loved (and counted on) help always being right there when she needed it. If she got stuck, she could ask her parents, Rose's parents, or even Auntie Jackie in an emergency. If anything went wrong with her Kindlings, they were there with suggestions to get her back on track. The only thing she always got right were her strategies. Once she had all the information, forming the best plan to get her Kindlings together came naturally to her. It was like a magical light bulb in a maze turned on and gave her a spectacular aerial view—she could see every possible outcome and pathway to get her to the best possible Singe scenario.

"No, you're not," Rose said, dismissing her pessimism with a hand wave and then asked, "And the second?"

Her parents exchanged a look. "Let's focus on one at a time, okay?" Aunt Tanya said. "A representative from the Oracle Council will be here to talk to you today. And then your Red Letters will arrive sometime between eight tonight and the next two weeks."

Every Matchmaker received their Kindling assignments by Red Letter courtesy of the Oracle Council. Once dispatched, it would continue magically appearing in annoying and inescapable places until opened by its Matchmaker.

"And there's one more important thing you should know," Uncle Norman said. "If you fail the first challenge, you'll have to wait an extra year before you're eligible to take your Flyer exam. If you fail the second as well, you'll be stripped of your magic."

"What?!" Rose shouted while Cora asked quietly, "They can take away our magic?"

"Calm down, calm down," Aunt Tanya said with a gentle smile, hands out in front of her. "I've never heard of that happening before. The Oracle Council just wants Fledglings to understand how important these challenges are and to take them seriously. They expect you to pass. They wouldn't have given you this opportunity if they thought otherwise."

Rose was asking a million questions, joy and excitement practically leaping out of her pores. Meanwhile, Cora felt like a giant boulder had just been placed on her shoulders, further weighing her down. She didn't feel ready to tackle a solo Singe, let alone her Flyer exam at all.

"Um," Cora said, getting up from her chair, "I forgot, I need to finish my math homework. I'm going to go do that." She ran out of the kitchen before they could stop her and headed for her room—a room that wasn't even really hers.

There was a nice desk, her laptop, a closet full of her clothes, but no pictures on the wall. None of her snow globes or magnet souvenirs or her endless collection of colorful pens. The bed was the only thing that felt like hers. She'd taken over the borrowed guest room, one soft pillow at a time.

Cora immediately picked up Scyther—her official

Matchmaker guidebook to help them study and train. On the outside, it was an unassuming hardcover book, dull brown in color, with no writing on the cover or spine. The inside was where the magic happened.

At precisely one hundred blank pages long, the information within their guidebooks could only be retrieved by asking the perfect question. A Matchmaker had to touch the cover, ask what they wanted to know, and the book would reveal the correct entries once opened. Bonding with their guidebook and asking it questions were specific skills they had to master because guidebooks liked being tricky. One wrong word, one stray thought, and it wouldn't hesitate to have a little fun . . . at their Matchmaker's expense.

Some guides were worse than others. Scyther had a chill vibe and never gave Cora any real trouble. She imagined it sounded like a condescending computer AI when she asked the wrong question: *Are you sure this is the inquiry you desire?*

Rose had named hers the Beast because it was like a demon bound to paper. It twisted just about everything she said, leading her on wild-goose chases through its pages.

Setting her intentions, Cora telepathically asked Scyther how being stripped would work. The answer came through immediately—no detours, no jokes or sass.

Contrary to popular belief, Matchmakers are not purely magicians. Matchmakers are born with the inherent ability to channel energy to serve their purpose, which manifests in various ways.

When Matchmakers complete a Singe, they are given the energy that it generates as a thank-you with a clause to pay it forward. Matchmakers don't exist without their Kindlings.

Cora had cleverly nicknamed that power *sinergy*.

*Singe* plus *energy* equals *sinergy*. It hadn't quite caught on with everyone else yet.

She continued reading:

At the discretion of the Oracle Council, a Matchmaker can have their channel permanently closed or, in some extreme cases, forcibly removed entirely. The process is colloquially known as being Stripped.

Cora's mom usually never answered her phone because she was so busy . . . and this time was no different. She settled for leaving a voice mail, pacing around the room as she spoke: "Hi, Mom. I know you're probably working, but I was wondering if you could call me? I don't know if they told you—oh, actually, you probably already know, but, um, they're making me do this challenge thing? Do I have to? Could you make them take it back? I don't think I'm ready to do this, but Rose is, obviously, so I think I got included, but no one *asked* me. . . ." She had to stop to take a deep breath. "Could you call me, please? I really need to talk to you."

Cora felt like she'd been lumped in by association. It wasn't because *she* was special—they only included her because she was Rose's cousin. And now she could possibly lose her ability to even be a Matchmaker because of it.

Her stomach hurt, twisting itself into knots as tangled as tree roots. She sat on the bed doubled over, trying not to panic.

"Everything okay?" Rose called while knocking on her door. "Auntie Jackie is downstairs."

Cora took a deep breath—inhaling and exhaling with her eyes closed. "Coming!" She knew she had no choice. All she could do was move forward. Because if she didn't, she'd be left behind.

Again.

# Chapter 3

Auntie Jackie drove Rose and Cora to and from school every day.

Minus the days when Rose had swim practice. That was too early for just about everyone in her family. After collecting a suddenly grumpy Cora from her room, they headed down to the parking garage, where she was already waiting for them.

"Good morning, girls," she said as they got in the car, Rose in the front and Cora in the back seat.

"Hi," Rose said.

Rose wasn't entirely sure what a hippie was but had a feeling Auntie Jackie might be one. She liked to wear loose, flowing clothes and mellow colors; free love was the movement; and her makeup looks came straight from 1960s magazines that had models with names like Twiggy on the cover. She even had large eyes just like her.

"You'll *never* guess what just happened," Rose said.

"I'm pretty sure I can," Auntie Jackie said as she drove out of the underground parking garage and onto the street.

"Oh. They told you already." Rose deflated a little, bummed that she wouldn't be able to brag about the challenge.

"It's unsurprising, for the most part." She glanced up at the rearview mirror. "I figured it would happen sooner rather than later."

"I'm so excited!" Rose was bursting with anticipation. "A solo Singe? *Gah!* I can't wait to get started. It's literally all I ever wanted. I am *so* ready for this."

"Good for you," Auntie Jackie said. "Hold on to that feeling because you're going to need it."

Cora sighed loudly in the back seat while continuing to stare out the window.

"Why is everyone being so negative?" Rose tried hard not to pout. "It's like you guys don't want me to be excited. This is a big deal for us."

Ever since Cora moved to Hotel Coeur six months ago, they'd been an unstoppable matchmaking duo. Rose knew she was great on her own, but Cora (and her awesome strategies) made her *fantastic*. They'd been so good the Oracle Council *noticed* and decided to reward them for all their hard work. Was she really the only one who saw it that way?

"Oh, I understand," Auntie Jackie said. "And it's okay to be excited, but there's still so much you don't know about the Matchmaker world that your parents are trying to shield you from. These challenges are one of those things."

Oftentimes, Auntie Jackie filled in the intentional blanks Rose's parents left. They never ever lied to her, but Auntie Jackie made sure Rose had the whole story. Her parents were like Cora's parents—super loyal to the Oracle Council. But Auntie Jackie had "history" with them, apparently. The kind of history no one talked about no matter how many times Rose asked.

Auntie Jackie continued, "Here's what your parents didn't tell you: the Oracle Council wants you to fail."

Rose blinked at her for a few seconds before laughing nervously. "That's not true. Why would they want that?"

"Because failure, specifically at their hands, keeps you in line. They want you to know who's in charge. They want you to know who has the power to control your fate. And they need to sow that fear as early as possible because they want you to remember it forever."

"Sounds fake, but okay." Rose laughed again. Her parents never lied, but she didn't think the same thing of Auntie Jackie. Some of the stories she told . . . they absolutely had to be made up. Or super embellished. "I'm not going to fail. I don't even know what that means."

"That confidence is exactly what they'll use against you." She glanced up in the rearview mirror. "And they'll use your doubt against you."

"Huh?" Cora blinked at her in confusion as if she hadn't been listening, but Rose knew she had been.

"Your doubt," Auntie Jackie repeated. "How afraid you are of being alone. They're not going to let you shrink yourself and hide behind your cousin forever. They want you behind *them*."

Rose turned around as far as she could, until the seat belt dug into her chest. She knew Cora had been having a hard time being away from her parents and moving to San Francisco, and her flaky friends back home kind of ditching her, and not having new friends yet, and . . . Oh. "Since when are you scared of being alone?"

"I'm not." Cora shook her head. "I feel like that's something I would know by now," she said dryly. Only she could use a tone like that and manage to not sound disrespectful. It was a gift.

Rose grinned at her cousin. Of course Cora wasn't lonely. Rose would never let something like that happen. "I don't care if they want us to fail or not. We're not going to. Right?"

"Right," Cora agreed, before looking out the window again.

★ ★ ★

Mae Jemison Private School hosted all grades, kindergarten through twelfth, split between two campuses. Rose and Cora went to campus A because the administration thought it'd be a *great* idea to lump kindergarten through eighth together, instead of giving the middle school students their own campus. Like they deserved. On non-swim days, they met up with Rose's best friends, Amber and Christine, in front of the school under the tall oak tree.

They weren't Matchmakers and didn't know Rose was one either. Keeping her abilities a secret was one of the Oracle Council's strictest rules. She wasn't supposed to talk about it, even though Matchmakers were literally everywhere, all over the world. Super unfair. Didn't they understand that best friends weren't supposed to keep secrets from each other?

"Guess who's going to bomb her history test?" Christine said with a bitter smile. Like everyone else at school, she wore her uniform as required but decided to go for a mermaid vibe on top of it. She added fake pearls galore—a headband, necklace, and a bracelet. Even her blond hair fell in effortless beach waves that took at least an hour to achieve.

The entire student body had quietly decided to all establish their own vibe, too. Cora had her rainbows, usually knee socks. Rose went for a more subtle celestial approach, sticking to a star necklace and silver rings on her fingers.

Amber said, "It's just one test. You'll be fine." Her theme was honeybees—a bee brooch, rings, and a yellow-and-black-striped tie.

"No, it won't. Grades are such a scam. Like, if I get an A plus, my overall average barely moves, but if I get a D, it gets shot straight to Hades. My mom is going to be so mad."

"Don't forget to pay the ferryman," Cora muttered, gently kicking at an exposed tree root.

Amber laughed awkwardly. "What did you just say?"

Cora said, "Nothing." She pasted the fake smile she always wore at school onto her face. Actually, calling it a smile was generous. It looked more like a reluctant grimace.

Rose poked Cora in the thigh. She'd lost count of how many times they'd had the *same* conversation:

*"They don't laugh at my jokes. They laugh at* me.*"*

*"No, they don't. GOD—why are you always like this? You won't even give them a chance."*

*"It's not like they give me one."*

*"They do! Every day! They try to talk to you, and you shut them out!"*

Cora said, "I'm going to head to class. See you inside," and walked off. They had the same first period.

Rose really wanted Cora to be friends with her friends, but it didn't seem like that was ever going to happen . . .

which made zero sense because Christine and Amber were amazing. They'd met on the first day of swim-team try-outs in sixth grade and had been best friends ever since. Seriously. They all made the team, and Christine said, "You guys wanna be best friends?" and that was exactly what they became.

Didn't Cora see how funny, overdramatic, and thoughtful Christine was? And how optimistic Amber was—whenever Rose had a bad day, there was Amber to automatically cheer her up.

Rose's connection to her Matchmaker magic ran deep inside of her. If she closed her eyes and concentrated, she could even hear it whispering about her past, her destiny, her birthright. She was born for this—to connect hearts all over the world.

So why couldn't she connect the hearts of her cousin and her friends?

Amber said, "I'm telling you she hates us."

Rose shook her head. "No, she doesn't."

"Then why does she act like . . . *that*? It's been like half a year."

"I don't think she does either." Christine took her back-pack off and began to search inside. "I think she just wants to find her own friends but doesn't know how."

"Maybe she's scared." Amber shrugged. "I used to be like that."

Cora didn't have trouble making friends. She *had* friends in Reno, after all. Maybe the way they treated her now made her afraid to try again. Their crappy rejection must have messed with her confidence.

Rose asked, "Do you think she's lonely?" She couldn't help but think back to what Auntie Jackie said. Did Christine and Amber notice it too?

"I don't know," Christine said, and then handed her a piece of paper. "But I was thinking maybe she could join this. You said she's really good at planning and stuff, right?"

Amber looked over Rose's shoulder and said, "Ooh! That's a good idea. We should ask her about it at lunch."

Christine said, "We'll need a plan, then. We can't just say: 'Hey, we think you don't like us so go make your own friends.' What do you think, Rose?"

"Umm." Rose clutched the bright orange flyer for the School Engagement Committee in her hands. She wasn't sure. It might be time to give their baby bird Cora a little push out of their nest to find her way. She could always come back if she wanted, of course, but flying on her own for a while wasn't a bad idea.

Cora might not be lonely, but she wasn't happy either. "Okay. Let's do it."

In the middle of planning, the school bell rang, summoning them to class. They agreed to text each other when they could and then finalize before lunchtime.

Rose didn't hate learning, but outside of swim team and seeing her friends, she didn't see much point in actually going to school—as in the concept of being forced to stay in a dedicated building for over eight hours a day. Uncomfortable seats, harsh fluorescent lighting, strict bell schedules that barely gave her enough time to get from class to class. The sheer amount of homework was horrible. Group work was devil work. Crowded bathrooms, endless gossip and rumors and scandals. She'd rather spend her time anywhere else.

Lunch was bearable though.

In the cafeteria, she plopped theatrically into the empty seat next to Cora. Christine and Amber followed suit. The Usual Suspects taking their usual seats.

Christine exchanged a look with Rose, who then nodded.

"So, Rose," Christine began, "you know the dance sign-ups are today after school, right?"

"Oh, right. Yeah," Rose said on cue. "I've been meaning to talk to you about that, Cora."

Cora looked surprised. "Me? Why?"

"Because you're perfect for it, of course."

Amber said, "Remember the Spooky Picnic we went to? The elementary kids planned it for us, and now it's our class's turn to plan something for the upperclassmen. They picked a dance."

"As if they don't already have enough of those," Rose added.

"Homecoming, winter formal, spring fling, prom," Amber said. "So unoriginal."

"Anyway," Rose said, "they need responsible people who are super good at planning to join the committee. That's you."

"Me?" Cora asked skeptically. "Um, when exactly am I supposed to have time for this since we work at the *hotel* now."

She meant matchmaking training, but Rose refused to take the bait. If she could be on the swim team, Cora, who was way more organized and addicted to studying than she was, could join the School Engagement Committee to make some friends.

"I think you'll be fine," Rose insisted.

"No. I don't think so." Cora shook her head for good measure.

Rose said, "At least go to the meeting. If it sucks, you can leave."

Christine said, "We'll go with you. If you need us to."

Amber said, "Yeah, totally. I mean, I'm not joining, but I can sit through a meeting no problem."

Cora looked at each of them, one at a time. Rose smiled at her, trying to be encouraging, because her cousin looked upset.

*Uh-oh.* She only ever looked like that when she was really, *really* frustrated and trying to pretend she wasn't. Like she was two seconds away from crying and yelling at the top of her lungs, but Cora *never* yelled. Her feelings just sort of boiled inside of her like a pot of hot water until they evaporated away.

Rose began, "On second thought, maybe—"

"Fine," Cora said, abruptly standing and picking up her lunch tray. "But I can go by myself."

# Chapter 4

Today was turning into an unbelievably bad, no-good kind of day.

First, Cora was being forced to complete challenges that could potentially put her entire Matchmaker future at risk. And now, she was very clearly becoming a pity project for Rose and *her* friends.

*We'll go with you. If you need us to.*

Maybe Christine didn't mean it in a bad way, but it hit her like a bolt of lightning. She was so helpless and pathetic that she needed a chaperone. Babysitters.

If they didn't want her around anymore, they could've just said so, instead of pretending like they cared with some stupid plan to make her go away.

"You don't have to walk with me," Cora said. "I can find it on my own."

"Of course I do." Rose grinned. "Of course you can."

This might have been Rose's idea, but Cora was determined to make it her own because she *was* good at planning. She'd prove them wrong—maybe she'd even be amazing at it. Maybe everyone would love her and want her to lead the whole thing.

Cora wasn't nervous or anything like that. At least not yet. Walking into the room might be a different story. She took a deep breath and tried to press her fear down until it was golf-ball-size like her mom had taught her. *I can do this. Everything will be fine. I can do this*, she thought to herself.

Rose continued, "I think ninety percent of your problems are confidence-based."

"No, they're not." Cora glared at her.

"*And* I think it would be a good idea for me to give you a little boost. Just enough to take the edge off so you have a good time." She wiggled her fingers in the air.

"That's not allowed." They weren't supposed to use their powers on each other because the Oracle Council said it was a waste of sinergy. Their powers were supposed to be used for other people who needed help.

Rose laughed. "No, it's 'frowned upon.' There's no actual written rule that says we can't," she said. "How about a makeover charm? Ooh, no, wait! I'll do *Belle of the Ball*."

Cora's eyes widened in horror. "Have you lost your

mind? Why would I want *that*?" She could practically feel the hives ready to itch their way across her skin. *Belle of the Ball* would amp up her natural radiance (which liked to hover at a nice -9.2) and make her the center of attention— like an actual magnet that would catch everyone's eye. They wouldn't know why, but they'd want to talk to her even if it was just to say hi and then walk away. Attention like that would lead to small talk, and small talk led to word vomit, and that *never* led anywhere worth going.

"Why not? It's an easy and stress-free way to meet people."

"Meeting people isn't my problem."

Rose's smile fell a tiny bit at the corners. "So, does that mean you do actually have a problem?"

Most people thought Rose was stuck-up, mean, and kind of pushy.

And sure, okay, they weren't exactly 100 percent wrong about that, but Cora knew better because sometimes she could see emotions. They started appearing to her shortly after she moved to San Francisco.

For Cora, they appeared to her in vivid images, helping her understand things in a different way, usually through nature. Her cousin's heart was *and* looked good—shots of clear sky filled with fluffy clouds right before a perfect rainstorm. She was sensitive and complex like a thriving tide pool shining in the moonlight and longing for the ocean.

She cared a lot. And she cared about Cora the most.

Even though the day felt horrible, being mad at Rose (and her gigantic shadow) wouldn't make her feel better. Cora took hold of her cousin's wrist. "I don't have a problem, okay? I'm still adjusting."

Cora promised her mom she would at least try to like San Francisco and her new life . . . but it just seemed impossible. Almost everyone she cared about felt so far away. She missed her parents and her house and her friends, who were having fun without her. They used to sit on bedroom floors playing games, making dance-challenge videos, and laughing until her stomach hurt, and they were still doing those things without her. She knew because they posted about it online. Her parents too—her mom started a travel blog full of her and Cora's dad exploring all these cool-looking cities while they worked. Their lives continued like Cora had never been there in the first place.

Cora had plenty of confidence, but sometimes she thought that maybe she wasn't worth keeping, that she wasn't worth remembering. She wasn't lonely—she'd been forgotten.

But she didn't want to tell Rose that. So, she said, "Being here is like being on a different planet. Even the air feels different. Thicker. And everything and everyone moves so fast. I feel like I'm constantly playing catch-up, and no one will slow down to be with me."

"But I'm here," Rose said.

Cora shrugged. "I don't know how to explain it, then, I guess. It's not you. I'm talking about *me*."

Outside the classroom, Rose wished her good luck. Cora knocked on the door before entering, and as soon as she did, the teacher greeted her.

"Hi, are you here for the committee meeting?"

Cora nodded and walked toward an empty desk. The room was only half-full, maybe ten or fifteen people. Not a single familiar face in the bunch.

The board behind the teacher read: *Mrs. Bond, School Engagement coordinator and English teacher.* She had olive-toned, sun-kissed skin with overly rosy cheeks, and wore a pair of flared jeans and a light, billowy blouse. Her hair was pulled back into a low ponytail.

"Welcome, everyone," Mrs. Bond said. "You can never have too many helping hands, so I'm glad to see a good number of you this time. Dance planning is harder than most people think. First order of business: we'll break down into subgroups. It's a fairly informal process." She passed out a sheet of paper to everyone.

Cora scanned it quickly—there would be three subcommittees in total: Location and Decorations, Tickets and Advertising, and Supplies and Entertainment. Each group would have to vote for a leader, who would be required to check in with Mrs. Bond three times a week outside of the weekly meetings where everyone had to be present.

Mrs. Bond continued, "We'll also need two people to be chair and vice chair who will oversee the entire event. They'll be responsible for creating a theme and keeping everyone on track."

Cora could practically hear Rose: *That's you. She's talking about you because you should be chair.*

"Why don't we break into groups now?" Mrs. Bond said, and gave instructions for where each group should meet in the room. "If you're interested in one of the chair positions, come see me and we'll talk."

Cora pressed her lips together and thought about her options. Did *she* want to be chair? Could she even handle something like that? She still had regular homework and Matchmaker training *and* independent study. Would she even have time for this? And not forsake her precious twelve hours of sleep?

But here, on the committee, she could pretend that she didn't feel so out of place and out of step with everyone. Being chair, she could make a name for herself without having "Rose's cousin" attached to it. She could make her own friends here.

Before she could think herself out of it, she jumped out of her seat and headed toward the front of the room. Someone beat her there. A short white girl with yellow hair—actually dyed sunshine-yellow hair—was already talking to Mrs.

Bond. Cora stood off to the side trying to listen to see if there were any questions she'd have to answer.

"Cora, right?"

Cora whirled around in surprise, hand on her chest and eyes wide. "Um, yeah?" She had no idea who he was, with his clear, golden-tan skin except for the one lone pimple on his chin, and dark curly hair that tumbled across his forehead.

"Rose's cousin from Reno who likes to wear rainbows?"

"Yeah, that's me. 'Rose's Cousin from Reno,'" she deadpanned.

"Sorry." His eyes locked with hers, sending an electric shock straight to her heart that had just calmed down. "I'm Dylan. Are you going for chair too?"

"Maybe. I wanted to ask some questions first."

"Same. I've never really been in charge of anything before." He lowered his voice and leaned in closer to her. "I'm honestly a little nervous, but I want to try, you know?"

The nerves in Rose's stomach began rattling like an almost-empty container of jelly beans. Dylan was close but not too close and . . . extremely cute. "I do. Yeah."

"It seems like it could be fun."

"Yeah. Totally."

"And I have a lot of ideas for the dance. For the theme and stuff."

"Oh," she said. Somehow Dylan having ideas snapped her out of the cute-boy reverie she'd been trapped in. She looked away quickly to clear her head and asked, "Like what?"

He squinted at her, a crooked smile out in full force. "Are you trying to steal my ideas?"

Dylan wasn't being serious, but she decided to answer that way.

"No. I'm still really new here, and I don't know what anyone likes or what kind of events have been planned before. If you have a really good idea, it might be better for me to ask to be vice chair so I can support you."

That's essentially what she did with Rose, and she liked their dynamic. Supporting and planning made Cora happiest. Being in front didn't make someone extra special or powerful. People who liked standing to the side could be important too. And besides, she *chose* who she wanted to stand by. She wasn't some mindless zombie sidekick.

"Oh. That's really nice of you," he said. "Maybe we could present a united front, so she'll take both of us?"

"Well, I still haven't heard your idea yet," she teased. "You have to impress me first."

"Oh yeah? I think I might be able to do that." Dylan hadn't stopped smiling since he started. Dropping his voice to a conspiratorial whisper he said, "I want to do a bait-and-switch. Everyone will think they're coming for a dance, and there'll be dancing because we have to sell it, but then we turn it into a murder-mystery party."

"That could be really fun."

"I know, right? I'm thinking about calling it the Masquerade of Winter Dreams. Have you read Edgar Allan Poe?"

Cora shook her head.

"That's okay," he said. "So, my idea is we'll start it as a masquerade ball with costumes and masks and then halfway through someone commits a murder. Everyone will have to work together solving clues to find the culprit."

"You may officially color me impressed. I'm partial to green. Emerald, not lime."

He laughed quietly. "Really?"

"Yeah! I mean, it's definitely a step up from the Spooky Picnic, and I had a good time there," Cora said, brain kicking into planning mode. "Have you thought about how you want everything to play out? We could have the committee and maybe even the chaperones be performers to make it interesting, since we'll have to be there anyway. It'll be our job to kick off the mystery *and* to keep it going. There's enough of us. Oh, and we should get prizes."

"Definitely need prizes."

"I agree," Mrs. Bond said, smiling. Cora hadn't noticed that the yellow-haired girl had left, and Mrs. Bond had been paying attention to them. "Sounds like you two have everything just about figured out, but I'd love to hear more."

After they finished telling Mrs. Bond, she explained Dylan's idea to the class. She held a quick vote and . . . Dylan and Cora officially became chair and vice chair for the upperclassman celebration. When the meeting adjourned, Dylan caught up with Cora outside.

"So, we should probably exchange numbers?"

Cora peered at him, pretending to be suspicious. "You want my number?"

Dylan nodded. "Only for official dance business."

"Uh-huh."

"Really. It'll be easier to brainstorm and check in and . . . stuff." He laughed.

Holding back her smile was a lot harder than it should have been. "Yeah. I'm one hundred percent sure the only reason why we'll ever text each other will be for official business."

"Exactly." Dylan seemed to be having the same problem. "We're in an official agreement for official business."

Cora laughed, shaking her head as they continued down the hall. Maybe she'd been wrong about it being a bad day after all.

## Chapter 5

From now until I ascend,
I promise to meet the expectations of
the Matchmaker Oracle Council.

Later that afternoon, Auntie Jackie escorted Cora and Rose to Hotel Coeur's lobby.

Rose's mom met them at the elevator with a big smile on her face. "Ah, finally! Come on, come on." She hurried them forward while pointing at the front desk, where an absurdly tall white man dressed in all black stood next to Rose's dad. He carried a briefcase with the silver emblem for the Matchmaker Oracle Council on the front.

"That's him," Rose's mom said.

Cora asked, "Him who?"

Auntie Jackie stopped in her tracks. Her face twisted into an angry frown, lips smashed together and eyebrows touching. "Edward," she practically growled.

Rose said, "Uh, I guess that means you don't like him?"

"There's nothing to like." She exchanged a cryptic look with Rose's mom. "Why did they have to send *him*?"

"Probably because he wanted to see you."

Rose's attention ping-ponged between them, back and forth, smile growing wider while trying to catch a single stray detail. Auntie Jackie kept most of her past vacuum-sealed inside a suitcase stored at the bottom of the ocean. She wasn't even really their relative—she'd been friends with Rose's mom since they were four, so they called her Auntie out of respect. It bugged Rose that they spent so much time with her, that she helped with the training and genuinely cared . . . but Rose didn't know much about her. She didn't even know where she lived.

Auntie Jackie scoffed and began walking away. "Bye, girls. Good luck and remember what I said."

Her mom asked, "What did she say?"

Rose shrugged. "A bunch of stuff." As long as it wasn't something serious, Auntie Jackie said it was better if what they talked about stayed between them. Advice wasn't serious. "What do you think we'll have to do?"

"I honestly don't know. I didn't get a challenge. No one in my generation did. You two must be very special." She smiled, bright and proud.

Cora groaned. She was practically dragging her feet.

Rose threw an arm over her shoulders. They were *exactly* the same height. "Can you at least try to see the positive side? Please?"

"Which is?"

"We are only two challenges away from becoming Flyers before *everyone else* in our generation."

Cora side-eyed her. "You don't care about everyone. You just want to rub it in Julien's face."

"There's also that," she admitted.

Julien Swift was the absolute worse. Rose's almost-archnemesis. *Almost* because if she gave him the full title, she'd have to acknowledge he was on her level, and she simply refused to believe that. The Oracle Council was *clearly* confused when they made them share the Wunderkind title.

Excluding Cora, he was the first Matchmaker she'd met in her generation because his family had been long-term residents at Hotel Coeur. Their parents kept pushing them together, trying to make them be friends. Rose *hated* it. He was always trying to prove he was better than her at *everything*. So annoying.

They even went to the same school until his family moved to New York last year. She'd thought she was finally rid of him, but no. Nope. He was still haunting her from across the country like a recurring nightmare she couldn't dream herself out of.

Rose's dad gestured to them when they got close. "Here they are," he said to Edward. "This is my niece, Cora, and my daughter, Rose."

"Hello," he said, leaning down to be eye level with them. His round glasses didn't have arms but were somehow perfectly balanced on his nose. "Do you know who I am?"

They answered, "Edward from the Oracle Council," at the same time.

Edward cocked his head to the side. "Hmm." He stood up tall again, turning to Rose's dad. "Do they do that often?"

Her dad said, "When they feel like it."

"They don't look alike."

"No."

"Not all twins do."

Her dad crossed his arms. "I don't know who started that rumor, but it's obviously not true."

Rose frowned—why were they talking about them like they weren't standing right there? Of course they weren't twins. They weren't even born on the same day.

Edward held up his hands in surrender, turning back to the girls. "I'm assuming your parents also told you why I'm here."

Rose answered, "To talk to us about the challenges."

"Right. The Oracle Council was quite pleased to hear you accepted their offer—"

"Wait, we had a choice?" Cora asked.

Rose nudged her in the side. "Of course we accept."

Edward continued, "Before you receive your Red Letter, I need to perform a small test. Think of it as a routine physical at a doctor's appointment."

"*Are* you a doctor?" Cora challenged.

"In a way. But only for Matchmakers. Rose, do you mind going first?"

Rose grabbed and squeezed Cora's hand before following Edward into the office behind the front desk. He closed the door.

"So," Cora began as she took a seat at the round table situated in the corner, "how do you know my auntie Jackie?"

Edward hesitated for a split second too long as he placed his briefcase on the table. "Who says I know her?"

"My mom. Auntie Jackie. Your body language." She laughed.

"Perceptive," he said as he sat down. The briefcase opened with a *click*, latches popping straight into the air with a flick of his thumbs. "We used to work together."

"Doing what?"

"This. Evaluating Fledglings."

That made sense. It explained how Auntie Jackie always knew so much.

A white machine that Rose had never seen before lay flat inside the briefcase. There were gears, buttons, switches, and vent holes all over it. There was a small black screen in the center with a blinking cursor. Edward placed a plain notepad and pen next to it.

"Can you hold out your hands for me?"

When she did, he snapped a white bracelet on each of her wrists and connected them to the machine with a short cable. They felt cool at first, then warmed up as they turned purple.

"Very good."

Rose asked, "What is that?"

"It's a device that helps me measure your aptitude," he said. "Your magical level, your channel, your overall state. We want to make sure you're in tip-top shape before you begin your challenge."

"How does it work?"

"I'm going to ask you some questions, and all you have to do is answer honestly. Sound good?"

Rose nodded. "I'm ready."

"Can you please state your name and age?"

"Rose Seville. I'm twelve." She peered at the machine expectantly—nothing happened.

"Very good. Now, can you tell me a lie?" he asked. "Any kind will do. You could say the sky is green if you'd like."

"Lima beans are the most delicious food in the whole world."

Edward laughed as the machine *clicked* and *popped*. He pulled a lever—and a short burst of steam puffed out like a mushroom making her jump. "Very good."

"Is it supposed to do that?" she asked nervously.

"It is." He fiddled with a few of the switches and pressed precisely two buttons. "Okay, Rose. I want you to tell me how it feels when you use your magic."

Rose thought about it. "Kind of cold, I guess. I get goose bumps and chills sometimes."

The machine didn't react, but he scribbled something down on the notepad, using symbols she'd never seen before. Definitely not English.

"And how do you access it?"

"What do you mean? I just use it."

"Could you elaborate on that?"

"On what? I think about using magic, and I can. It just happens."

Edward opened his mouth and closed it. He must have decided to ask her the next question telepathically because he kept staring at her. No blinking. No moving. Just staring at her for so long, she noticed the tiny flecks of green in his blue eyes.

Rose began to feel uncomfortable—a prickly feeling creeping up the back of her neck. She usually got it when her parents found out about something she did that she wasn't exactly supposed to do. Like that time she skipped school with Amber and Christine and went to Chinatown.

"You"—he paused, pressing his lips together—"you think about using magic, and you can perform it."

"That's what I said."

"It doesn't feel like you're, um, *pulling* it from somewhere. For example, let's say you're at school. Your teacher asks you to put your textbook on your desk, so you open your backpack and retrieve it. Then you can use it. Does it feel like that?"

"No. Is it supposed to?" she asked, suddenly worried.

Magic had always been easy for Rose. Her parents never said anything about it. Auntie Jackie told her that it was effortless for some Matchmakers, that it was a good thing.

Edward's face didn't look like he thought that at all. It looked like she just told him she got bit by a rattlesnake and needed to go to the hospital right away. Finally, he said, "Usually. That's very interesting."

"Good interesting or bad interesting?"

He gave her a quick, tense smile and flipped another switch on the machine. "Just interesting. I'm assuming you're aware of where our magic comes from. How it's stored?"

"Of course. My parents explained it to me when I was three after I cast the equivalent of a Dazzling charm on my babysitter."

"I've heard stories about that. Would you mind telling

me what happened, in your own words?"

Rose didn't remember that *exact* conversation. She relearned the process during training. It just sounded really impressive when she bragged to other Matchmakers about channeling when she was three years old.

Every Matchmaker could channel the energy generated from a successful Singe—referred to as magic, more often than not. They captured and absorbed it into their bodies, storing it like fireflies in a jar until they were ready to use it.

The test to become a Fledgling was simple. On their fifth birthday, they were given a tiny bit of magic to see what they instinctively did with it: channel or let it dissolve.

But sometimes, it didn't work like that.

Rose leeched magic from her parents without their knowledge. It was raining that day, and she really, really, *really* wanted to go outside. She remembered smiling at her babysitter, and off they went. No umbrella, no rain boots, no jackets. They had stomped in rain puddles for almost half an hour in the courtyard before anyone noticed.

The problem was, raw magic like that—not bound by the intent of a charm, enchantment, or a spell—quickly slipped into mind control. Her babysitter didn't even know *how* they'd gotten outside. Representatives from the Oracle Council showed up hours later to investigate. Rose didn't remember getting in trouble, but she thought her parents had.

Something similar happened to Cora. She failed her first channel test but leeched from her parents three years later. They figured it was a family thing.

After Rose finished explaining what happened, to the surprise of no one, Edward said, "Very good." He pressed the largest red button on the machine. It began to power down with a soft whine before going silent like a TV did when it turned off—a barely audible *wink*.

"I'm going to be honest with you, Rose. I don't know what I expected, because your reputation very much precedes you. I can see why the Oracle Council selected you for this challenge. Your stats are very impressive."

"I have stats?" Rose asked, perking up. "Can I see them?"

Edward laughed. "Yes, you do. We all do. And no, you cannot. This particular device isn't capable of measuring someone as exceptionally gifted as you are. But from what I've read in your file and after talking to your parents, I have every faith that you will do well." He removed Rose's wristbands and rested them on a hook inside the briefcase.

"Can I ask a question, then?"

He nodded.

"How often does the council pick Fledglings for the challenge? My dad said once in a blue moon, but I think he's just saying that because he doesn't know. And my mom said no one in her generation got one."

"Their answers were true enough. Sometimes we'll go generations between challenges, and other times, like now, there'll inexplicably be three."

Rose's left eye twitched. "Three?"

"You, your cousin, and Julien Swift."

"Julien." Rose sounded exactly how Auntie Jackie did earlier when she saw Edward. Maybe he was *her* Julien. Suddenly, she liked him a whole lot less than she did thirty seconds ago.

*Of course* they offered it to him too. She should've known.

This was supposed to be *her* moment. Hers and Cora's. Not hers, Cora's, and Julien's.

"Interesting." Edward looked amused, a slight smile tugging at the corners of his mouth. "He had a similar response to finding out you had been chosen as well. You two are quite the pair, I hear."

Rose bristled, metaphorical feathers ruffling to the high heavens. "We are *not* a pair. Not even close."

Chapter

6

Edward stood up when Cora entered the room. "Please have a seat."

She sat in the chair he pointed to, and when he asked, held out her hands. He placed a white wristband on each wrist. They slowly changed colors to green.

"Very good," he said. "This device was designed to test your aptitude and ensure you're at an acceptable level to complete your challenges."

Rose had bounded back into the lobby, both excited that she passed and seething because Julien had also been chosen. Cora wanted to melt into a puddle like a snowman left to fend for itself in the hot sun. Everything made even *less* sense now. How in the world did she get lumped in with both Wunderkinds? Just . . . *how*?

Cora slumped in her seat, shoulders hunched. "Could you try to not look disappointed when your machine tells you I'm not like my cousin? I'm kind of sensitive about it."

"This is about you, not Rose," he said kindly. "Let's begin—can you please state your name and age."

"Cora Seville. Twelve."

"Very good. Now can you tell me a lie? It can be anything. For example, you could say the sky is green."

"The sky is green."

Edward glanced at her—quick as a mouse dashing across the floor—before turning his attention back to his device. "Are you comfortable?"

"I'm fine."

Steam hissed and erupted out of the machine, pluming upward before evaporating in the air. He had to flip several switches to make it stop. "Interesting."

Carefully Cora asked, "Is that normal?"

"It's not abnormal." He pushed a small red button on the back of the machine. "I'd like you to tell me how it feels when you use your magic."

Cora began to drag her teeth across her bottom lip, thinking and frowning. "It was . . . hard at first. I have to concentrate a lot and close my eyes to visualize it. My mom taught me how to use reflective rumination to focus, so I do that too. It's a little easier now. I'm not as fast as Rose."

"Your mom taught you? Interesting. What do you see?"

"I see me, usually, except I'm all lit up like a Christmas

tree. I have to focus on the lights, what they look like and how many I want to use, and then they float away. When I open my eyes, I can use my sinergy."

"Sinergy?"

"Oh, um, singe energy. Sinergy. It's what I call my magic."

Edward laughed unexpectedly, and Cora relaxed the tiniest snail-size bit. "I like that. Very creative."

The machine began to whistle, low and insistent. He made it stop with one hand and wrote something on his notepad with the other.

"And how do you feel when you use your sinergy?"

"Good but also weird. Warm and cold at the same time. Kind of tingly."

"I read in your file that you were previously classified as a late bloomer and later a leech before becoming a Fledgling. That's quite the rare combination."

Cora wanted to collapse in on herself like a dying star. She still remembered every detail about the day she failed her channeling test. Her dad looked confused. Her mom started crying. The Oracle Council representative told her she was a late bloomer—that her channel either wasn't open or didn't exist yet. She needed more time.

When she'd asked what that meant, they said she would be tested again when she turned ten. If it wasn't open then, it was doubtful she'd become a Matchmaker.

It was the worst day of her entire life. Nothing had ever topped that moment.

She started praying every night for her channel to open. Every shooting star, every time they drove through a tunnel, every snapped wishbone, every birthday candle, every fallen eyelash—she always made the same wish: *Please, please let my channel open.*

It took three years' worth of wishes for it to come true.

Cora wasn't sure how she did it, but on an unbearably hot day, she randomly pushed enough stolen magic into a dollar bill to make the ice-cream-truck lady give her two Popsicles instead of one. Her mom had come running outside because she felt someone leeching magic from her. She had no idea what Cora had done until the Oracle Council called.

The machine began to make a loud *whirring* sound like something inside it was spinning too fast.

"Does that make you uncomfortable?" Edward asked, pressing the small red button again.

Cora shrugged. She wasn't sure what she was supposed to say, so she kept quiet. So far, the machine had puffed steam, whistled, whirred. She thought each one must mean something different.

"Okay. Let's talk about something else. I don't know if your mom told you this, but reflective rumination is actually an advanced skill. Most Matchmakers don't learn

it until their fifteenth year. Do you use it to visualize anything else?"

Something inside of Cora told her not to tell him. Her
parents didn't even know about the things she could see
now. She'd been waiting to tell them in person, not over
the phone. "No."

The machine blew a gasket—literally. Something popped
off the top and shot straight up to the ceiling. Steam poured
out of the device, surrounding them in seconds.

Edward stared at her, eyebrows raised.

Steam must have meant the machine knew Cora was
lying.

"When I said no, I actually meant . . . sometimes." She
held her breath—the device settled down, only chugging a
little bit. Yep. Definitely for lying.

"Could you share with me how?"

"I could."

"Will you?"

"It's still kind of new. I don't even know how it works.
I can just . . . see stuff sometimes."

"Like?"

"I can see plans. If I'm researching my Kindlings, there's
a moment when everything comes together. I can . . . *see*
it. All of it laid out in front of me. So, if I choose to go this
way"—she pointed to the left—"I can kind of guess what
will happen. And if I don't want that, I can go the other

way. Does that make sense?"

Edward stared at her, silent and unmoving as a statue. "It does," he said quietly. "Have you told anyone you can do that?"

"Just Rose."

"Your parents don't know? Your aunt and uncle?"

"No."

"I'm going to advise you to keep it that way. For now."

"Is that bad?" Suddenly, it felt like rocks were tumbling all the way down to the pit of Cora's stomach. "Is it cheating? I only use it to help me plan my Singes. That's all. I *swear*."

"No, no, it's not cheating. Calm down. It's . . . unique."

Cora nodded, hoping it was okay to believe him.

"Is there anything else?"

"Maybe."

Edward lunged forward, pushing the button before the machine reacted, and gave her an expectant look.

"Yes," she admitted reluctantly. "Sometimes, I can see people's emotions if I touch them. All people, not just Kindlings."

"How long have you been able to do this?"

"It started when I moved here, so six months, I guess."

"What does it look like? What do you see?"

"Nature. Plants and weather and stuff."

"Would you mind demonstrating this for me?" He

placed his hand palm down on the table.

"Oh, it doesn't work all the time. Just sometimes," Cora warned. She touched the back of his hand and closed her eyes. "Uh, there's nothing. Oh, wait, no, it's just dark and cold. I can't see anything until lightning streaks across the sky. I'm in a forest with all the trees cut down. It's sad and lonely here. I think the lightning feels like hope."

Edward moved his hand away quickly, jolting Cora from the scene. "Okay. Very good. I've seen enough." He removed the wristbands, placed them on hooks, and closed the briefcase. "I'm going to be honest with you now, okay?"

Cora fidgeted in her seat, pulling her shirtsleeves down over her hands. Part of her wanted him to say she failed, that she wasn't eligible for the challenge and would have to wait until she turned thirteen like all the other Fledglings. But another part of her, a very small and fragile part, hoped for something she wouldn't allow herself to think about.

"Okay," she said, staring at her shoes.

"I have some concerns about you participating in the challenge. You don't have the level of control over your, uh, sinergy that I usually like to see in Fledglings. However, I can see that you're very determined. Previous testing has shown you to be proficient with your guidebook already, which is very impressive. I'm going to allow you to proceed."

"Really?" Cora reacted so fast it kind of hurt her neck.

"Really." He nodded.

Cora jumped to her feet, ready to tell Rose that she passed, and was halfway to the door when he called her name.

"One last thing," he said. "I'll have to follow up with your parents and the council regarding your visualization abilities. That will most likely result in me returning for more testing, which is probably for the best anyway. The challenge is going to be very, very difficult for you. This way, I'll be able to check in on your progress."

"Oh, okay. Perfect." She smiled politely as she waved goodbye, but inside, she was screaming.

Instead of walking back to the lobby, Cora decided to sneak behind a row of decorative plants, hang a left, and head toward the ballroom hallway. Hotel Coeur had four ballrooms—Chamber, Venus, Echo, and Stardust—each designed with gigantic crystal chandeliers, art deco cornice molding, carved pillars, and hardwood dance floors. They were usually rented out for weddings, special events, and the occasional work conference.

Cora loved the Venus ballroom the most. Everyone did—it was so popular it tended to be booked years in advance. That day it was empty, but the round dining tables and chairs from a prior event hadn't been put away yet. She sat at the closest one and put her head down on the table.

Using sinergy, magic, had never been easy for her. Edward didn't need to tell her it would be "difficult." Rose could use hers all the time for anything without even thinking about it. That's why Cora studied so much, why Scyther was practically glued to her side, why she helped Rose plan her Singes—she *needed* to practice.

Their matchmaking styles were complete opposites. Rose relied on magic like 99 percent of the time. Meanwhile, Cora preferred a more down-to-earth approach—her cousin called it "old-fashioned" and said it was like "using a dictionary instead of the internet."

That was such a weird thing to say because Cora *did* use the internet. A lot. She located her Kindlings through research, finding out everything she could about them online before moving on to real-life reconnaissance; determining the best place to have a matchmaking meet-cute and flawlessly establish a Connection by saying their name; and for a short while, become the best part of their lives. After reading her Kindling's heartstrings, it felt more fulfilling to dive into their lives, talking to them, really getting to know them one-on-one.

Cora knew she should practice her charms and enchantments more, but she didn't want to become too reliant on magic. Whenever her dad asked her why she was so reluctant to use her sinergy unless it was absolutely necessary, she always gave him the same answer: balance. Magic could be fleeting and fickle. She wanted to find a balance that worked for her because she would still have her brain if her magic ever failed.

Her phone vibrated in her pocket. It was probably Rose, wondering where she went. Cora gasped in surprise—it was Dylan.

DYLAN: Hi checking in on official business only.

CORA: Sorry the number you have texted is no longer in service.

D: Oh.

C: The owner has decided to run away from all her responsibilities to live with penguins in Antarctica.

D: Guess that means you haven't started your homework.

C: Penguins are surprisingly anti-studies.

D: They always seemed so curious to me.

D: Everything ok?

C: No. Yes. I'm fine.

D: Do you want to talk about it? I'm a good listener and reader. :)

C: Why did you call me Rose's Cousin from Reno today?

D: Because that's how I knew you.

C: I love Rose but I really don't like it when people do that. It happens a lot.

D: I won't do it again.

D: Are you mad at me about that?

C: No I'm not mad. But that's kind of why I'm upset. Something else like that happened today but worse.

D: Who did it? I'll beat them up.

C: Ahaha no violence please but thank you.

D: Tell them that anyone who makes you upset has to answer to me.

D: I'll watch out for you.

C: . . . Why?

D: I pictured you being really sad and wanted to help.

D: I can't actually fight haha if anyone ever messes with me my brother takes care of it.

C: What's his name?

D: Damon. He's in tenth grade. Do you have any brothers or sisters?

C: No I only have Rose.

D: Did your parents give you similar names on purpose too?

C: How are they similar?

D: Four letters, two vowels and two consonants that alternate.

D: And they both remind me of the color pink.

C: Gotcha. Her name is actually Roseanna. Mine is a secret.

D: ??? What is it?

C: Nope.

D: Oh, come on you can't just say that and not tell me.

C: Sure can. Nope.

D: Please???? I really wanna know.

C: Fine but you have to tell me something too.

D: Okay. Secret for a secret. You first.

C: No you. You gotta give me a good faith payment.

D: Last year I got bit by a radioactive spider and have been a high-flying vigilante of justice ever since.

D: You never said it had to be a real secret. Your turn. :)

C: Technically. Legally. My name is Coretta. I made the smart decision to shorten it in third grade.

C: Cora just feels more *me* you know?

D: Yeah. I do.

D: I really like your name. Both of them.

## Chapter 7

Rose had fully expected to wake up to her Red Letter the day after Edward gave her the council stamp of approval.

That didn't happen. Not that day or the next, and the wait was turning into pure agony. Now here she was, almost a week later and still no Red Letter, practically disintegrating from anxiety. How could they make her wait like this? She was *ready*. This was a thousand times worse than waiting for her birthday. A million times worse than waiting for her parents to wake up on Christmas Day.

Rose unplugged her hair straightener, slipping it into its carriage to cool safely. She liked to straighten her curly hair to make it longer and more manageable whenever she could. Which was usually on non-swim days. She'd been doing it by herself for a couple of years now, ever since she begged her aunt Iesha to teach her how during one of their visits. Rose's mom didn't really know how to comb her hair because it was a different texture than hers. But that was okay. Her mom did other stuff with her instead. Like today, her parents were taking her and Cora out for a fancy brunch, courtesy of one of her mom's clients.

Hotel Coeur had been in the Seville family for decades. Her dad had been the twin who volunteered to keep the family business going. And when Rose's parents got married, her mom outright refused to work there. She wanted to keep her own career, eventually landing on divorce lawyer—a controversial occupation among Matchmakers. The Oracle Council must have approved because almost all her clients coincidentally became her Kindlings. It was like her mom always said, *A settlement with a side of Singe never hurt anybody.*

Her phone buzzed on the counter. Julien had sent her a message.

JULIEN: Rose.

ROSE: Nemesis.

J: Why do you insist on calling me that?

R: What else should I call you?

J: I don't know. My name might be good.

R: Pass.

J: Whatever.

J: Did you pass your rep exam?

R: Naturally.

**J: Did you get your letter yet? I got mine today.**

Rose almost dropped her phone. A shriek of epic pro-portions began building in the back of her throat, but when she caught sight of her wide eyes and shocked expression in the mirror, she swallowed it back down. After taking a deep breath, she smoothed her hair one last time and stomped out of her bathroom, all the way down the hall and into her parents' room.

With all the dignity and drama she could muster, Rose threw herself facedown on their bed. And *then* she screamed.

"Oh, stop being so ridiculous," her mom said, laughing. "It'll happen."

Rose wasn't surprised that her mom knew why she was upset. She'd done this at least twice a day for the entire almost-week she'd been waiting.

"No, it won't," she cried, voice muffled by the blankets. "They lied to me. They're not giving me a challenge."

"I told you it could be up to two weeks, honey."

"Yeah, but I didn't think that would actually happen."

Still fully immersed in her drama, she sat up and took a deep, heaving breath. Her mom sat at the vanity inside her walk-in closet doing her makeup.

"Julien got his."

Her mom blinked in surprise. "How do you know that?"

"He texted me to *gloat* about it. He's just a gloating goaty-goat boy."

"Oh. Honey, no." Her mom's laughter made Rose smile. "Don't call him names. Especially ones that terrible. You're more creative than that." She winked.

Rose's smile got bigger. "Okay. I'll get some tips from Cora." She slid off the bed. "What time are we leaving?"

"About twenty minutes."

That meant forty minutes. Whatever time her mom said, they knew to double it. "I'm gonna go downstairs, then."

"Don't bother anyone. Let them work."

"Saying hi isn't bothering people."

"Roseanna." Her mom pointed at her with a mascara wand. "No charms, no magic."

"Fine. You're no fun," she muttered, walking away. All she did was create a couple of *Causing a Commotion* charms to create an impromptu dance party in the lobby one time and suddenly she's a *bother*. Everyone had a *great* time! It boosted employee morale! But did her parents appreciate that? Of course not.

Rose loved the energy that vibrated in the air throughout the lobby. It had so much potential. It was the perfect place to talk to new people, perfect for "accidental" meet-cutes in the elevators, staged love-at-first-sight catastrophes in the waiting area, and first blush of friendships in the dual bookstore giftshop.

Quickly, she passed under the trellis entrance to the café. It had been designed to invoke a certain Parisian feel, inspiring love and light in between scones and smooth coffee. She popped behind the counter to make a cup of hot chocolate. Technically, she wasn't supposed to do that. Her parents had ordered her to stand and wait in line with the guests, even though she didn't have to pay for whatever she wanted.

But was it her fault that she knew how to make hot chocolate better than all the baristas?

No. Besides, she'd be quick. Hummingbird quick. In and out before anyone noticed.

The door to the kitchen swung open. "Hey, brat. Stealing again?"

Samantha. Before she could stop herself, Rose glared at her.

Her grandma used to say something about flies and vinegar and honey—Rose could never remember exactly—but the gist of the meaning was to be nice. She could do nice. She would be so sweet cavities would worship her as a goddess.

"Good morning," Rose said, sweetly as sweet could be. "Your multiple piercings are looking extra shiny and rebellious today."

"You're so weird." Samantha laughed, unleashing her infamous crooked grin.

"Thanks," Rose said, reluctantly putting back the hot chocolate ingredients. So close, yet so far. "I try."

"Since you insist on being back here, restock the pastry case, will you?" Samantha asked.

"Pass," she said. "You can't just flash your beauty queen smile and bat your fake eyelashes to make people do whatever you want. It's a good plan, I'll give you that, but it doesn't work on me."

"They're not fake."

They were so fake. Only camels had lashes that long.

Samantha finished wiping the counter and rested against it. "Princess Brat is at it again, I see. Too good for manual labor when your parents don't order you to do it?"

"You get paid. I don't."

"A nice person would have noticed I'm on shift by myself and helped me because it's the right thing to do. But no, not you. Whatever, spoiled brat." Samantha winked at her mockingly before moving on to help a customer.

Rose's face flushed with heated anger. Samantha somehow always managed to cut too close to a hurtful truth.

She wasn't spoiled. And she *was* nice. She hated when people assumed they knew anything about her when they obviously didn't. She began cracking her knuckles to keep herself calm—one of her worse habits. But not even the usually satisfying *pop* could settle her boiling temper.

"Time to blow off some steam," she whispered to herself.

Time to do some good with a little bit of chaos.

Tiny acts of matchmaking chaos were her specialty.

As long as she didn't cause a scene, her mom wouldn't get mad. Probably.

Keeping an eye on Samantha, Rose folded a piece of receipt tape into a small paper airplane. She wrote *Run away with me* on one of the wings, planted a kiss on the other, and infused the whole thing with a pinch of magic. Picking up her abandoned hot chocolate cup, she turned it upside down and taped the airplane to the bottom.

Once the cup was filled and then emptied, the person who drank it would be hit with an urge to invite that *oh so special* someone in their life to go on an adventure. All the *Runaway* charm needed was an open heart to seal the deal.

"I saw that." Rose's dad stood on the other side of the counter with his arms crossed. While Cora was Aunt Iesha's mini-me, Rose didn't really look like either of her parents, but she did have her dad's mischievous, Grinch-like grin.

"Saw what, Daddy?" she asked, all innocence—he never made her throw her airplanes out. "I didn't do anything."

"Uh-huh," he said. "Your mom is ready to go."

After Rose walked from behind the counter, her dad wrapped an arm around her shoulder and led her out of the café and toward the parking garage.

The restaurant was in Sausalito, about thirty minutes away from the hotel. It was one of Rose's favorite drives because they had to take Highway 1 to get there, which meant driving across the Golden Gate Bridge. Even Cora, who pretty much hated all things SF, loved the bridge. Water stretched endlessly in both directions. Dozens of people walking and riding bikes on the pedestrian pathways. The way the breeze picked up especially on days when the fog rolled in—and continued to hover, even in the middle of a sunny day.

"Cora," Rose's mom asked, "how are the dance plans coming along?"

"Pretty good. We've finally settled on a date and an agenda. Me and Dylan have been working on the story together. We want to get it perfect before we show it to Mrs. Bond."

"Ahh, Dylan." Rose couldn't help herself.

"It's not like that."

"Oh yeah? Who are you texting right now?"

Somehow Cora managed to drag her gaze away from her phone long enough to glare at Rose, who said, "That's what I thought." Rose giggled—Cora and Dylan had been texting nonstop since they met. "There's no way you're brainstorming all day and all night. No dance needs *that* much planning."

"We're friends," Cora mumbled.

"Uh-huh." Rose snapped her fingers. "Oh yeah, don't you have something you need to ask my mom?"

Cora sighed loudly.

"Dylan asked her out on a date."

"It's not a date! He just wants to hang out today," Cora said. "He knows I just moved here and he's just being nice."

"Hang out where?" Rose's mom asked, concerned.

"At the pier. He wants to show me around."

"Oh, that's perfectly fine," she said. "We can drop you off on our way back into the city, and Norman can pick you up when you're ready."

"Yeah," he said, "I'll make sure to get a good look at him for your dad."

*"We're friends."*

Rose sang, "Just two friends going on a not-date."

"Whose side are you on?" Cora hissed.

"I'm on the side of love," Rose said. "Any Matchmaker worth their heart-shaped mole can see he has heart eyes dancing up and down his sleeve every time he looks at you."

"He doesn't," Cora said, trying to hide her smile.

"He does. Don't try to act like you don't see them either." Rose grinned. "Aren't you glad Christine came up with the idea for you to join the committee?"

Rose was sure being a Matchmaker was her destiny.

Even when she wasn't using her magic, she created perfect pairs. She was only teasing Cora because it was her sworn duty as a cousin and a best friend. She honestly didn't care what they decided to be in the end. Dylan made Cora *happy* right now, and that made Rose happy.

A sound like a match striking tinder sizzled and sputtered in the car. The smoky smell of an extinguished flame wafted around them as a Red Letter appeared directly in Rose's lap.

Rose screamed, "Holy crap!"

Her mom shouted, "Language!"

Her dad, who was driving, turned his head to look at Rose, and Cora shouted, "Eyes on the road!"

Her dad said, "I'm gonna pull over. Hold on! Hold on!"

Rose picked up her Red Letter, running her fingers over the embossed lettering.

> Attn: Roseanna Seville
>
> Challenge in the First by order of the Oracle Council

"It's time," she whispered. Her heart practically climbed into her throat. "It's really happening."

Her dad took the next exit and ended up stopping in a random grocery store parking lot. Rose held up the letter for Cora to see as if she weren't sitting right next to her.

*"Look at it."*

Cora laughed. "I know what a Red Letter looks like."

"But this one is extra special. Challenge in the First. Wow." Rose gasped. "Yours must be on the way soon too."

"Let's hope not."

"Don't be like that," she whispered, trying not to cry. "This is good for us."

"We know we can't help you, sweetie," her mom said, "but if you wanted to open it now, we wouldn't stop you."

Rose nearly laughed. Both of her parents had turned around in their seats and looked as anxious and excited as she felt. And they looked proud—so, so proud of her. Eagerly, she flipped it over, sliding her fingers under the wax seal. The small white card inside smelled like roses and had inlaid gold-colored swirls.

### SAMANTHA JULIETTE EVANS

Deadline: Fourteen days from the date of receipt

Cora leaned over to read the card and said, "Uh-oh," with a laugh.

Fledgling Red Letters *always* listed two Kindlings. Even among the fully initiated, only experienced Matchmakers, the best of the best, were given solo-Kindlings. This was the real deal.

But *Samantha*? Really? Not that Rose would let the fact that Samantha was her almost-archenemy stop her from performing her matchmaking duties, but it seemed like an odd choice. All of Rose's Kindlings had been total strangers in the past. She'd never had to match someone she knew before—it made her instantly curious. Would the process feel different? Could she really work with someone she didn't like? Everything about this assignment would be new territory for Rose.

The Oracle Council really was testing her. Or setting her up—Auntie Jackie's warning replayed in her mind. Fourteen days. They'd given her two weeks when time limits are practically unheard of.

Well, if this was how the Oracle Council wanted to play it, she was suited up and ready to go.

"I got this," she said with a grin. Her hands stayed steady as she passed the card to her parents.

"*Oh,*" her parents said in unison, and her mom added, "Oh, dear."

"You certainly have your work cut out for you." Her dad passed the card back to her. "But if anyone can do this, it's most definitely you."

"Right. Like I said, I got this," Rose repeated. "There's no way she'll be *that* bad. I can handle *anything* and *anyone.*"

Chapter 8

Brunch turned into a celebration in honor of Rose getting her Red Letter.

Cora thought everything tasted incredible. She had the fresh fruit tarts, ate a billion cheese blintzes, and even tried a smoked salmon quiche for the first time. Rose kept finding ridiculous ways to ask for a mimosa, but her mom refused to give in. Once, after she took a bite of toast with orange marmalade, she said, "Oh, wow, it's so tangy and . . . orange. I *love* oranges. You know what *else* has oranges in it on this fabulous Challenge-in-the-First Red Letter Day and is *great* for special occasions?"

Cora felt like a stuffed roly-poly bug by the time they left. She was dreaming of her bed and taking a nice, long nap when she remembered she was going to hang out with Dylan. Her aunt and uncle dropped her off at Pier 39.

"Have fun!" Rose shouted from the window. "Don't be

afraid to use a charm or two if you need it!"

"No, no, don't do that," her uncle said. "No magic."

That was a weird reaction. Cora never used her sinergy outside of a Singe anyway. "I wasn't planning on it."

"Good. You don't need it." He glanced at the dashboard clock. "I'll meet you back here at seven. Be safe."

"I will."

Cora waved them off and set out to find Dylan. He waited for her near the sea lion rocks—there were so many of them there! Brown and floppy and happily sunbathing.

"They're so much bigger than I thought," Cora said. And not to mention loud. She heard them barking all the way from the street.

"Wait until you see an elephant seal. Those things are huge."

"Are they here too?"

He shook his head. "Pretty sure they're in South Bay."

"I have no idea where that is." Cora laughed. She took a few pictures of the sea lions on her phone to send to her parents.

"Would it be okay if I take some pictures of you? My brother loaned me his camera." He held up a super professional and expensive-looking one. "It's kind of my hobby."

"Um, sure." She posed in front of the railing with the sea lions in view.

"Thanks," he said. "So, are you ready to be a tourist?"

As they made their way around Pier 39, Dylan took her picture *everywhere*. The ferry terminal; in the archways of each pier entrance; in front of Alcatraz, even though it was just a tiny blip in the distance surrounded by water. He even paid for her to get a caricature sketch done—and took pictures of her while she posed for the artist.

And honestly? It felt kind of weird at first. Dylan didn't make her feel uncomfortable or anything. She just wasn't used to someone being so intensely focused on her. On top of that, all the photos turned out *amazing*. Even the ones that caught her mid-laugh, mouth wide and smiling. It was like he had some kind of internal Instagram filter magic. Cora barely recognized herself in some of them.

She looked so . . . *alive*. And happy. Not at all awkward like she did in her selfies or when Rose forced her to have a photo shoot.

After they stepped onto the giant gold carousel, he pointed to the green sea dragon. "How about this one?"

"Sure. He seems friendly enough," Cora joked, climbing on its back.

"And he's green. Emerald, not lime." He snapped more pictures of her and, when the ride stopped, helped her down. "How do you feel about ice cream?"

"Hot take but they're not all created equal. There is such a thing as bad ice cream."

"Follow up: How do you feel about chocolate?"

"American chocolate is gross, and I usually won't eat it."

"Seriously?"

"I'll name names and everything wrong with each one. There's a list," Cora said. "I take my chocolate consumption *very* seriously."

Dylan laughed. "How does Ghirardelli rank? It's my favorite, and the shop isn't too far from here."

She pretended to think about it. "I'd be willing to reconsider it on those grounds."

To get to Ghirardelli Square, they had to walk up what Cora had dubbed "murder hills." The kind of hill that pushed your flimsy muscles to the limit and made your lungs fight for every gulp of oxygen. The city was full of them—sinister slopes of death around every corner. Angles so steep even some cars struggled. Walking uphill was a balancing act involving leaning forward so far, one wrong step and you'd fall flat on your face. And walking downhill really meant running because gravity insisted on taking over. Fortunately, this was a mini one, and she didn't disgrace herself by wheezing like a deflating balloon. Dylan sped up a little to beat her to the door and held it open for her.

Inside, there wasn't a line. They walked right up to the cashier. After Dylan ordered, he said, "And whatever she'd like. Go ahead."

Cora had heard that boys were supposed to pay for

everything, but that didn't make sense at all. She didn't want him to assume that she expected him to do that. She also wanted him to know that she could buy stuff for him too. Her parents called each other partner instead of husband and wife, and said they were equals. This was equal.

Not that she was going to marry Dylan or was thinking about marrying Dylan or anything like that. Besides *Dylan* hadn't said it was a date. They were just hanging out . . . as equals. As friends.

Before her parents left, they set her up with a bank account and her very first debit card. Every month they deposited money in the account just in case she wanted to buy herself something fun. Having the card felt like a huge responsibility, so she rarely used it.

The cashier handed Cora a number plate. They chose a table outside on the patio because it wasn't as crowded.

"So, what do you think so far?" Dylan asked.

"I think the ice cream better be worth the hill we had to walk up to get here."

He snorted a laugh and shook his head slightly. "I meant about San Francisco. Are you feeling better about it? There's lots of good stuff here."

"I mean, I don't hate it. It's just different."

He smiled at that, a tiny dimple appearing on one corner of his mouth. "Things will get better if you make the most of it."

She made a face. "You sound like my dad."

"Believe it or not, you're not the first person to say that to me." He grinned for a moment before making a seriously concerned face and pitching his voice deeper. "How's school? Are you thinking about joining any more clubs?"

"Dad voice. Nice." Cora shrugged. "It's okay." She didn't mind being asked about school, but it wasn't what she'd been hoping for. Actually, she didn't know *what* she'd been hoping for. She just felt a tiny bit disappointed. "My classes are okay. My teachers are okay. Rose's friends are okay. Everything's just okay." Her hands fussed with the napkin dispenser. "Definitely a no for the clubs."

"Why?"

Rose's idea had obviously panned out, but Cora didn't want to press her luck. "Is there a nap club? I'd join that," she said. "My mom wants me to be on the swim team like Rose."

"And you don't want to?"

"Nope. I've seen Rose's workouts, and I watched a couple of practices. I'm not built for that kind of activity."

"Not to be cliché but: you never know until you try."

"Uhh, I do know. My lungs threaten to go on strike any time I even think about swimming. You were *this* close to hearing me wheeze outside after walking up that murder hill."

Dylan laughed again. "You're so funny."

"Thanks. I spend a lot of time writing and practicing my jokes in advance. Being effortlessly witty on the spot takes work. Dedication. Commitment."

"If that's the case, then I'm sure you could convince your lungs to be a team player," he said. "But I get it. Some things just aren't worth working toward right this second. I could be good at basketball if I practiced, but I like football and chess more, so I don't play, even though the coach and my parents won't drop it."

"You play chess?" Cora asked, a little impressed.

"I'm not good at it," he said, blushing a little. "I just like it. It's fun, and the club is pretty cool."

Chess. She could handle chess. Maybe. "Would they let a super beginner join? Like, could I start at checkers and work my way up?"

"That would be a first, but I think I can convince them to make an exception."

The waitress set their food down on the table. Cora ordered the Presidio Passion—vanilla ice cream with layers of strawberries and hot fudge, whipped cream, and a chocolate-covered strawberry on top.

"Okay," Cora said, still reeling from the first bite. "Definitely worth it."

Dylan went for the Treasure Island—it also had vanilla ice cream, hot fudge, and whipped cream, but added an entire brownie, chopped almonds, and a cherry.

While they ate, he asked her questions—her favorite movie, her best friend's name, her favorite animal, her favorite state, if she liked music—and she answered. It quickly turned into a game, as if he had to ask her the first question that popped into his head and she had to answer faster than the speed of light.

And when her brain couldn't stand it anymore, she looked away to reset, giving herself time to calm down. And every time her gaze felt drawn back to him, his was already on her. Cora realized it was because he didn't need to reset. She had his full attention because he wanted to know her.

Nothing stole his focus away—not the delicious ice cream or the shouting kids or the seagulls calling out overhead. He looked at her as if she were the only thing that mattered.

Suddenly, everything felt too close, too warm, too tight. Her heartbeat felt like it turned into hummingbird wings, fluttering in her ears. She looked down again at her half-eaten sundae, busying her hands with the spoon.

Rose had been right. It was obvious.

She'd missed it earlier because he'd been hiding behind her camera. Now with nothing between them . . .

Attentive. Kind. Smart and so cute. He loved music, had decent grades, a reactive sense of humor, and was quick to laugh. *Oh*, he had such a *great* laugh—melodic and contagious—and a fantastic smile too. That laugh could call the angels down from on high. It could force the pied piper into retirement (which was a good thing, considering the pied piper was a child abductor).

And she felt . . . good around Dylan. Like she could talk to him forever and never get bored of his voice or his smile. Like he understood her. When she got quiet, he did too—and it was okay, never awkward. He didn't expect anything from her.

*What does he see in me?* she wondered.

"Okay, big-question time," he said.

Her head popped up with no hesitation, ready and wanting to look at him again.

"What do you want to be when you grow up?"

Cora almost laughed. "I want to be like my parents. Do what they do," she said, deciding to tiptoe around the truth. "They work for a government-like entity, traveling the world and solving problems. Making the world a better and more loving place." She did laugh, then. "I know that sounds kind of ridiculous. Their job is kind of top secret. It's why I live here now and they don't. They couldn't take me with them for this trip."

"That sucks," he said. "Do you miss them?"

"Every day." Cora sighed. "What about you? What does adult Dylan's future look like?"

He sat back in his seat, thinking. "I don't think I know

yet. I like a lot of stuff, but nothing I want to commit to forever."

Matchmaking was her destiny. She couldn't even imagine life without that path laid out in front of her. Part of her wanted to ask him what that was like, but she figured he'd probably end up thinking she was weird.

"Hey, Cora?" he asked. "What time did you say your uncle would pick you up?"

"Seven."

"We should probably start to head back then. It's six forty-five."

Cora checked her phone. Her uncle had already texted her twice: once to say he was on his way and a second time to say he was waiting at the ferry terminal.

"How did that happen? I'm filing a complaint with the time lords." She texted him where they were because there was no way she was walking all the way back there.

"Time Lords don't control the flow of time."

"These ones do. Chronos manages them, or something like that. Tragic coincidence about the name similarity."

They placed their dishes in the receptacle and walked out together, Dylan holding the door for her again. She followed his lead down the hill, back to the Embarcadero, walking side by side. The perfect quiet settled around them once more.

It had been such a good afternoon. More perfect than

she could have ever thought to hope for. They'd say good-bye and she'd start checking her phone obsessively waiting for him to text, start counting the minutes until she saw him at school on Monday.

Cora had seen this play out hundreds of times since she turned eight and came into her powers. And now it was happening to her.

What a day. What a life.

It was hard to believe they had met only a week ago. It had felt like so much longer than that.

*Great*, she thought. *Romantic clichés are happening to me now too. Fantastic.*

Dylan's hand touched hers—a jolt of electricity shocked through her. First, the back of his hand, and then his fingers against her palm. She wanted to look at him, but she didn't dare. She held her breath as his fingers touched hers and slid in between them.

When he squeezed, she squeezed back.

DYLAN: Don't be so negative.

CORA: I'm not negative. I'm just . . . realistic. Grounded in reality.

C: My feet are planted so firmly on the ground I started growing roots years ago.

D: So you're a tree?

C: I could be a plant. Or a bush. I'm still in the early stages of conversion.

D: And now you're avoiding the subject.

C: I'm not. I *changed* the subject.

D: Ahaha at least you're honest.

D: They seem nice to me. Maybe Rose is right and you just need to give them a chance.

C: Amber is kind of scary. She stares at me like she's trying to read my mind like she's the thought police or something.

C: Christine is okay. I guess.

D: Maybe Amber is looking for a partner in crime. You give off intense mastermind energy. She wants to join forces but if you don't she has to figure out how to take you down.

D: Personally, I think they know you're super smart and funny, but your shy persona is confusing them. Maybe Amber thinks if she stares long enough she'll catch a glimpse of the real you and figure out a plan to make you more comfortable so you can be yourself.

D: I think they want to like you. Maybe you should let them.

C: . . . Do you have a bright side for everything?

D: No. Just for you.

## Chapter 9

Rose had always been an early riser.

Even if being on the swim team hadn't trained her to wake up before 5:00 a.m. during the season, she still preferred to greet the sun. Sitting in her window seat, swaddled in a quilt with a cup of hot chocolate (made in her kitchen, not the café), she watched as the black sky faded into blue before exploding with oranges and yellows. She filled out her journal, scheduling her days and month using stickers and sparkly gel pens.

*Swim practice*—Christine's mom drove them to swim practice and always showed up at the same time.

*School*—unfortunately.

*Cousin time.*

*Homework*—maybe.

*Red Letter deadline for Samantha*—usually always worked the morning shift.

*Cora's dance*—committee members not only got to attend the event they planned, but they were also allowed to bring two guests. Rose was ready to masquerade the night away.

If luck was on her side that morning, and it typically was, Rose would stroll into the café, establish the bond, and flit off to swim practice, all in less than thirty minutes.

Her alarm began to chime as if she needed it.

Throwing off her blanket, she turned on her music. Blasting it as loud as she dared, she sang and danced as she got ready. By the time she twirled into the kitchen, her mom stood sleepily at the counter, sliding an omelet onto a plate already filled with toast. She wore a plush red bathrobe, ratty black slippers, and crescent-moon patches under her eyes. Her weekend spray tan had washed off, leaving her grumpily in her natural pale state. She always slept with her hair in spongy pink rollers—hair that was currently ginger red after she'd spent about a year as a blonde.

"Good morning." Her mom yawned, covering her mouth with the back of her hand. She didn't have to get ready for work for another hour. Still, she woke up to make Rose breakfast every single morning before swim practice without fail. Kissed her cheek, her forehead, and wished her a good day before falling back into bed.

"Morning," Rose said, sitting down. "This looks really good."

Her mom peered at her over the rim of her cup of coffee. "Samantha's on shift today, if you happen to be looking for her."

"*Mom!*"

"*What?*"

"You can't help me," Rose said through her teeth. She glared for two seconds before returning to her breakfast.

Her mom only laughed, kissing her forehead again. "I'm *not* helping. I'm just saying. Just in case." She set her cup down on the counter and leaned against it. "Giving general information isn't helping. The schedule is clearly listed in the break room. Anyone could know that."

"I have to do this by myself," Rose insisted. She loved her mom and loved that she figured out a sneaky way to help in a small way—she'd learned about gray areas from her mom, after all. But she had to do this on her own. "Please."

Inside her middle elevator, Rose exhaled as long as she could, emptying her lungs until they protested. She leaned against the back wall, face upturned to the mirrored ceiling. Tiny little gray handbags had pitched a pop-up shop under her eyes. She hadn't slept well because she was wired with anticipation, and it showed—she looked *tired*.

This was her moment. *The* moment. Closing her eyes, she tried to make herself relax with more deep breaths and focusing. She wasn't scared. No part of her twitched or shook with nerves.

Rose smiled at her reflection. She was ready.

Samantha, as promised, had already begun working. A small line of people waited patiently at the counter for their turns.

Rose found a spot off to the side and near a rather large plant, where hopefully she wouldn't be seen or interrupted. Creating the Connection wouldn't require anything extra on Samantha's part. Kindlings didn't even feel the magic as it began to work.

Everything started with their name.

"Samantha Juliette Evans." Rose imagined a long metal chain to begin the Connection, eyes glowing purple. She sent it forward, flying toward her Kindling. Connections were soft and effortless as silk sliding across skin. She waited patiently for the familiar sensation of their hearts linking together to take hold.

But that didn't happen.

Rose had to grip a nearby chair to keep from falling over because Samantha, wiping down the counter without a care in the world, had pushed back. The imagined chain snapped back to Rose like a released rubber band after being stretched too far.

Samantha blocked Rose. She wasn't letting her in!

Did Rose just get rejected? She planted her feet while focusing her mind and setting her jaw. She tried again, carefully this time, making her magic feel unassuming by thinking of a thick length of velvety yarn. She would quietly slip in and knit them together—Rose rocked back on her heels. It felt like a large door had just been slammed in her face. She stood there, mouth agape and in shock.

It was true that some people could naturally repel Matchmakers. Usually, they had snark and sass to spare, and the ability to wield both like weapons. They pushed everyone away, even on a subconscious level. That kind of obstinance only grew and grew until it could even keep magic out. Rose had heard stories of it happening to Matchmakers, and remembered Cora showing her the entry in Scyther once.

Samantha began taking the order of a customer with brilliant blue hair. If Rose didn't make this Connection, she wouldn't be able to read Samantha's heartstrings, and if she couldn't read her heartstrings, she wouldn't be able to make a Singe.

No Singe meant she failed.

Failing meant . . .

Desperation swirled around Rose's intent, amplifying her power. Her hands were shaking, so she balled them into tight fists, anchors at her side. Sweat began to bead on her brow, and her chest rose and fell too quickly. *In through your nose, out through your mouth,* she told herself. *You can do this. You are Rose Seville. There's nothing you can't handle.*

Intention sharpened and honed to a point like the precise tip of an arrowhead, Rose focused on Samantha again. She visualized nocking her magic arrow, pulling back, and letting it fly.

Suddenly, Samantha turned to her left, staring directly at Rose.

The gaze they shared pulsed with understanding allowing Rose to see that Samantha's heart was covered in a hard, spiked shell. Rose kept pushing and pleading and fighting her way forward. *Let me help you,* she thought over and over. *You can trust me.*

A scene appeared in Rose's mind again—black and white, it felt like something small and wanting and afraid, like the last puppy left in a cardboard box, outside in the pouring rain.

The Connection was established. Rose had seen her Kindling's heart.

And she was in trouble.

Rose collapsed into the chair next to her and placed her head between her knees. She counted to ten, breathing in and out, and trying to calm down. Her stomach roiled with nervousness, her breakfast threatening to come back up.

"Excuse me, dear." A hand touched Rose's shoulder.

The voice wavered slightly, old and worldly. "Are you all right?"

Rose sat up, pushing her hair back and trying to smile at the old woman. "Yeah. I'm fine, thank you." Her phone began to vibrate. "I have to go though. Thanks again."

She picked up her bag and ran to the lobby door without looking back. She needed to take a second to catch her breath, to figure out *what* happened, to process if that was real. Could her Kindling really repel magic? Or was Rose just too tired, too off her game? She opened the front passenger door of the van and hopped in.

"Good morning," she said.

Christine's mom gave her a quick nod, hands tight around the steering wheel. Rose turned around—Christine looked worried, and Amber was sobbing.

"What happened?" Rose asked, which turned out to be the wrong question. Her head already hurt from establishing such an unstable Connection with Samantha, and Amber's wailing made it worse. The little bit of distance between them helped—it must have been torture being right next to her as she went full-on keening banshee. She knew Amber had good lungs, but the sounds she made should have been medically impossible.

"Check your phone," Christine said to Rose.

She did and . . . oh no. Jason, Amber's boyfriend of three months, broke up with her in four terse text messages.

"Amber," Christine's mom began, "maybe I should take you back home today."

"If I don't go to school, he'll know it's because of him and what he did." Amber sob-wailed for what felt like the hundredth time. That sound was going to embed itself in Rose's brain soon. Right when she thought she was free, in the middle of the night, as she was about to fall asleep, it'd come blasting through her subconscious to wake her up.

Christine said, "I don't think your plan is going to work the way you think it will."

"I can't let him win!" Her misery was so palpable, if Cora had been in the van, she probably would've been knocked straight into a coma without even touching her.

For a moment, Samantha faded from Rose's mind, quickly replaced by her friend's distress.

Amber didn't deserve to feel that way. She was a straightshooter with golden heart-shaped bullets who loved animals and fashion. If Rose ever needed help, Amber was the type of friend to show up leading the rescue calvary.

In this case, though, that guy just wasn't a good match for her. They all told her so. When Rose met him, his vibe screamed player—100 percent into himself and dedicated to finding out what he could get away with. The absolute worst of the worst.

"After I swim, I'll be fine," Amber pleaded. "Totally fine."

★ ★ ★

She was not fine.

In the locker room, Rose watched as Amber continued to sob in the corner. Hair still wet and dripping on her uniform, Amber began to hyperventilate.

"Man, she's really going through it," Jess, a teammate, whispered to Rose. "This is why I don't date. This is why I will never date." She walked away, shaking her head.

"I'll go get some more tissues," Rose said. On a very general, extremely basic level, she understood Amber's distress.

Heartbreak was like a diamond—a multifaceted phenomenon. It was physical, mental, and emotional. You're hurting for what was, what could have been, and what can no longer be.

Amber had convinced herself that he'd been the One. She was devastated about being *wrong*, not just about losing him.

. . . and it was time for her to get over it.

Rose couldn't heal Amber's heartbreak, but she did know a couple of Whirlwind charms, designed to help a Kindling rebound faster. Amber needed a heaping dose of distraction. Something to help her remember that it was Jason's loss, not hers. And maybe just a pinch of vengeance.

The answer came to Rose with a snap of her fingers: *Look What You Made Me Do* charm.

Whirlwind charms demanded sacrifice. A heaping dollop of magic mixed with a careless whisper. She had to infuse her will and wishes simultaneously, while holding them separately in her heart to stay in control. Complicated, thrilling stuff—it made her skin tingle from the challenge of it.

Rose sighed, admiring the slight shimmer now coating the small packet of tissues. "Ah, the things I do for friendship." Back in the locker room, she knelt in front of the still sobbing Amber. "Here. Use these."

Amber sniffled and gave watery thanks. Her fingers barely brushed the plastic before her eyes pulsed with purple. She gave a hiccupping gasp and whispered a tiny, *"Oh."*

"You're welcome," Rose said. Now, instead of sobbing through school, Amber would be strutting down the hallway like the main character in a movie with her own personal soundtrack.

Magical mission accomplished.

As always, it felt simply *amazing.*

Samantha's face flashed in her mind. Okay, so her Challenge in the First wouldn't be easy, but Rose didn't need easy. As long as it wasn't impossible, she could conquer it. Still, the Connection didn't *feel* right. Like it was blurry, existing but only partially. Not strong enough to hold in her mind, and certainly not strong enough to access

Samantha's heartstrings to begin finding her match.

Her next step would have to be the thing she hated most: consulting with her guidebook, the Beast.

In first period, American history, Rose sat near the front with Cora and quietly worked on forming her question. The last time she used the Beast, she asked for the name of the Matchmaker who held the record for the fastest completed Singe. It unironically gave her the entry for *Fall from Grace*—a charm meant to humble a Kindling too arrogant for their own good through a series of mishaps and unfortunate events. They'd become a catastrophe magnet for twenty-four hours.

Message received loud and clear.

Cora had thought that was hilarious.

Now, Rose scribbled a minimum of five different versions of her question in her notebook, whittling it down until it was as precise as she could make it.

In second period, English, Rose sat in the last row by the window and could turn her body so no one would see what she was doing. She closed her eyes, pressing her hands flat on the Beast's cover, which was yellow instead of brown like Cora's. Focusing on remembering the details, Rose thought of everything that had happened so far: the Red Letter with only one name, invoking the Connection, Samantha pushing her away, being reluctantly let in and seeing the heart of the resistance.

*What would be the most helpful thing to do for magic-resistant Kindlings?*

She hoped for a broad, overarching answer. A trouble-shooting *explain it to me like I'm five* list. Her camera won't turn on. Simple solution: check the batteries. Occam's matchmaking razor. She grimaced against the familiar *buzz* of the guidebook searching for the answer and the mildly unpleasant *zap* when it was ready. Holding her breath, she opened the cover, expecting the worst as she skimmed the page.

The Beast had generated a numbered list! Rose nearly squealed out loud in excitement. The page was full of all kinds of different charms, a handful of Sonic enchantments, and a risky spell called an instant-Singe.

An instant-Singe disregarded the five foolproof Singe steps and cut straight to the happy ending. But if a Matchmaker messed it up, disaster wouldn't be far behind. Failed instant-Singes almost always resulted in infamous enemies-to-lovers matches.

Starting tomorrow, Rose would park herself in the café and try every charm and enchantment the Beast recommended until something stuck.

And something would because Rose *refused* to fail. The alternative was simply too horrifying to think about. She would *never* survive the shame of having to wait an extra year to take her Flyer exam. They might even take away her Wunderkind title—oh god.

Julien? Beating *her*? Inconceivable. Unacceptable. It literally made her stomach have a cramp attack. No. Nope. Not happening.

Rose swore with one hand on the Beast that she would do everything in her power to make sure she came out on top.

CORA: Wait wait the culprit can't wear the peacock mask if the doorman does. It would be too obvious.

DYLAN: No, that's why it's perfect. Everyone will see them standing there, but did they actually? Walking in they don't know it's a mystery so they don't know they should be paying attention yet.

D: And the doorman would've seen everyone, giving them time to select the victims.

C: I really think people will be able to put that together too easily.

C: It should be one of the chaperones because they're walking around with rulers. They'll have the time and the motive if there are any couples who keep on dancing too close. They decided they should be punished. And since there's more than one person in the role, it'll make it that much harder to pinpoint who did it without it turning into a witch hunt.

D: Guilt by association could be a good plot twist. I still think purity police should be the red herring.

C: What if we used them both? One PP and the doorman working together then?

D: There you go, always with compromise. You know when you do it first, it makes me seem unreasonable if I say no.

C: Then don't be unreasonable. :)

D: Fine haha I'll make the changes to the master document.

D: I can't believe we have to present this to Mrs. B tomorrow. Are you nervous?

C: Nope.

D: I am. :(

C: Why? You wrote a great story and we know she likes it.

D: Presentations kind of freak me out. It reminds me of public speaking which I suck at.

C: I think you can do it.

C: And I'll be there too so if you mess up, we mess up together. I got your back.

Chapter

10

The lunch meeting with Mrs. Bond went by incredibly fast.

Just like Cora promised Dylan, she was 1000 percent on board with their storyline. She even praised their plot twist *and* the plot twist to the plot twist. They did have to make a few edits, like changing some of the character names—she wasn't a fan of Purity Police—and the timing of a few of the reveals to make the timeline of events stronger. Still, they had a plan. And she'd already shared it with the rest of the committee by email so it could be discussed for final *final* edits at the next meeting.

After that, the whole event would be announced to the student body. Cora's name, along with Dylan's, would be on all the advertisement posters, which was super cool. That might have been the part she was looking forward to the most, besides the dance itself.

Instead of heading into the cafeteria, they decided to walk around the perimeter of the school. Only upperclassmen were allowed to leave their campus, so they got stern looks every time they passed a yard monitor. Dylan had started telling her a story about a disastrous party he went to once.

Cora asked, "So let me get this straight: You went to the party and just hid in the garage the whole time?"

"I was by myself." He laughed. "J and J bailed on me. They talked me into it and then had the nerve to get food poisoning that morning."

J and J, a.k.a. Jax and Jill, his friends. All Cora knew about them so far was they were siblings with horrible reputations for skipping school, which is why she hadn't met them yet. "That sounds extremely plausible, yep," she said. "Almost as good as 'Sorry, I can't go out with you because I have to wash my hair.'"

He laughed. "They shared a bad breakfast burrito."

"Ah. I retract my snark, then," she said. "How come you didn't just leave? I mean, since you didn't want to be there."

He made a face. "I didn't want to be rude."

"And hiding in a garage was the opposite of that?"

"Hey, if anyone wanted to find me, I was there. It's not my fault no one was looking for me."

"Fair," Cora said. "Moral of the story: don't go to parties

where you don't know anyone when you have slight social anxiety."

"I wish you could've been there."

"You didn't know me then," she pointed out.

"I can still wish it." He shrugged.

"Well, if I ever build a time machine, I know what my first stop will be."

"Aww, you'd do that for me?" he teased.

Cora looked up at him. "I would."

He grinned at her for a few heartbeats before looking away. "Are you busy tonight?"

"Kind of?" She sighed. "There's some family stuff happening, so I have to be there as much as possible."

Rose had been not so subtly constantly freaking out about Samantha and her challenge. Samantha only worked in the mornings, leaving Rose with less than a few hours to work on her match. The previous night, she got into a fight with her parents because they wouldn't let her skip school to spend more time hovering around Sam.

She'd also been casting all kinds of charms nonstop, and using that much magic had started to wear her down. *Irritable* wasn't even the word. Grizzly bears would be scared of Rose right now. But whenever Cora offered to help, Rose said no: "I have to do this myself. Thanks, but no thanks."

Cora figured the best she could do would be to hover

around Rose, hovering around Sam. If her cousin needed her, she wanted to do her best to be there.

"Does that mean you can't hang out at all? 'Cause I was thinking of maybe asking my dad to drive us to the Academy of Sciences. If you were interested in that kind of thing at all."

"Uh, yeah. I love that place. When did you want to go?"

"Whenever," he said quickly with a huge smile. "Whenever you want."

"Okay. I'll ask my aunt tonight."

"Cool. I don't know why I always get so nervous to ask you stuff like that." He laughed again.

Cora was constantly surrounded by love of all kinds—studying, assessing, Singeing. She'd never really thought about what romance would be like for herself. They hadn't even known each other that long yet. She hadn't had time to really sort through how she felt. All she knew so far was: Girl met Boy. Girl made Boy laugh. Boy had a great laugh, and Girl wanted to keep hearing it. Spending time with him fell in line with that.

Cora knew she wasn't the daughter of the year. She wanted to be good, so she tried to be good. Even still, there were times when she fought with her parents. But she could never, ever imagine yelling at them the way Rose yelled at her parents. Not in a million years.

Everything was fine. They were having dinner. Talking about their days. All perfectly normal . . . until Rose brought up only going to school for half days when Samantha worked in the café again.

Her parents said no.

Rose exploded. Her voice got really high, and she started using her hands for emphasis. At one point, she accidentally grazed Cora's shoulder—sulfur, that rotten-egg smell, and slow-rolling lava appeared in her mind almost instantly. Her cousin was always so cool, confident, and in control. She hadn't realized just how much pressure Rose felt until she saw the volcano.

Cora didn't think they even noticed when she quietly got up from the table and slunk away to her room. It had been quiet for a while now. Rose left, probably going down to the lobby or kitchen to make some of her Chaos charms until she felt calm again.

After replying to Dylan's text—he sent her pictures of potential dance decorations submitted for approval—Cora grabbed Scyther out of her backpack. She sat in the middle of her bed, making a nest out of her pillows until she was comfy, and then thought her question.

*Is there a charm to help someone generate ideas?*

Scyther never hesitated with her. The answers always came quickly:

Not for you. Now turn the page.

Cora did—there was a new paragraph of text waiting for her.

Charms are a crucial element to any Matchmaker's arsenal. While the same hundreds of standard charms have been used for centuries, most modern Matchmakers have taken to creating their own.

Cora sighed. That wasn't what she asked. "But I don't want to do that."

A new sentence appeared underneath the entry—then it must be correct to assume that you do not wish to aid Rose Seville, after all—and quickly vanished. Scyther didn't sass her often, but when it did, it went all out.

"I don't even know how to design a charm from scratch, and I don't want to waste sinergy figuring it out."

No response.

"Hello? Are you not going to talk to me now? Fine."

This was what Edward meant when he called her proficient with her guidebook—she could "talk" to Scyther. If she asked a question out loud, it would sometimes answer.

If it felt like it. Usually, it didn't. She closed the book, reset her intentions, and thought a new question: *How do you make an effective charm?*

There are several types of charm classifications. The most common are considered Temptation charms, where the recipients are suddenly seized by an intense desire. Another common variety are Dazzling charms, which cause the recipient to be temporarily irresistible to anyone in their presence.

The Illumination class may be of particular interest to you. They consist of charms designed to provide clarity for their recipients. Occasionally, you will encounter Kindlings who are too trapped in their own heads to realize their heart's desire. These Kindlings will never see the signs, remain oblivious to obvious suitors, and will be, quite simply, doomed to never experience the possibility of what-if without direct intervention.

Illumination charms are often useful in a variety of situations.

"I *know* all that. What I don't know is how to make my own! Why are you being difficult today? You're never difficult."

**Things change.**

That much was true. Case in point: she was seriously considering using a charm to help Rose. If there was another way, she'd happily do that instead. Unfortunately, sometimes, magical problems required magical solutions. The charm wouldn't even work if Rose didn't want to have a breakthrough . . . but who wouldn't want to have a light bulb moment? Cora couldn't imagine someone saying no to simply getting *inspiration* to find a way to help themselves.

Or maybe she was just trying to convince herself she was doing the right thing.

Creating an original charm might be like making a Conduit. Those were easy. All she had to do was pick an object that represented something her Kindlings had in common, place their heartstrings inside, and seal it with sinergy.

She didn't *have* Rose's heartstrings though. Besides, she didn't want to give her a perfect match, well, a perfect *answer*. Rose said multiple times she wanted to do everything herself.

No, Cora didn't want to help Rose with her challenge. She wanted to help *Rose*, period, by reminding her cousin that she wasn't alone and unclouding her mind so the sun could shine on her.

Cora crept into Rose's empty room, heading straight for the desk, where her colorful planner lay open in the center. It wasn't a diary or a journal, and Rose even let her look at it before, so she didn't feel like she was snooping.

Almost everything important that month had been written in orange. Cora picked up the only two orange gel pens she found. Holding them tightly in her hand and against her chest, she closed her eyes—and imagined Christmas tree Cora on the first try. It was like walking into a dark, empty storage closet with only one source of light. Nothing else.

*Okay,* she thought, *I can do this. I want to make a charm for Rose.*

Cora never knew how much sinergy to take from her inventory, but something inside of her did. As she watched, three large ornaments turned from white to green. Together, they contained the amount she would need to make her charm. She pulled them off the tree, one at a time. Each one warmed her hands like perfect cups of hot chocolate on a cold winter day before she released them. They floated up and away, ready to be used.

When Cora opened her eyes, they glowed bright emerald green. She imagined feeling like a ship lost at sea, running out of hope and options, terrified of never finding her way. Just as she was about to give up, something caught her eye—there was a lighthouse in the distance! After combining her sinergy with her intentions, she poured the mixture into the pens.

"The light, the light," she whispered, "remember to follow the light."

The pens pulsed and sparkled, but it only lasted for a few seconds. They looked normal again, as if nothing had happened.

Her very first original charm, *The Lighthouse*, had been created.

She just hoped it would work.

DYLAN: Things that keep me up at night #22—once dolphins learn to speak human it's over for us.

CORA: Oh my god.

C: For better and for worse, I think of dolphins as the humans of the sea so you're probably right.

D: So cute, so untrustworthy.

C: Fun fact, orcas are dolphins not whales.

D: Oh man I really am right, aren't I? Those things hunt sharks for fun. We're doomed.

Chapter 11

In the morning, Rose made her way to the café with the Beast *and* Cora with her, for backup.

"You're actually standing in line. I'm amazed," Samantha said.

Rose replied, "Two hot chocolates, please."

Samantha stared at her for a second, probably waiting for a syrupy sweet retort. It didn't take her long to give up. She rang up the order and zeroed out the total. "It'll be a few minutes."

"Thanks."

Rose chose a table near the pastry display because Samantha would pass by her frequently there. She shouldn't have had to be next to her Kindling to tap into their Connection, but this obviously wasn't going to be a run-of-the-mill Singe.

"I'm glad you wanted me to be here," Cora said, yawning.

Expecting Cora to be up and functional a single second before she had to be was a herculean task, and Rose knew it. "Yeah. I really wanted to do it on my own, but I'm beginning to think that's not going to happen."

"I don't think there's a rule that says we can't help each other," Cora said. "They would've told us that."

"That's not what I mean. I just feel like, sometimes, maybe, impossibly, I don't know everything."

"Oh," Cora said.

"Yeah." All Rose's usual tricks weren't working. That morning while she was filling out her planner, she suddenly realized that thinking outside the box would be essential to her success. "I think it might be like Auntie Jackie said: they're using my confidence against me. I feel my best when we're working together, and they chose us for the challenge together. I've decided to take it as the obvious sign it is."

"Big sign." Cora grinned. "Neon."

"Shut up," she said playfully.

"You know they also chose Julien. Maybe we should—"

"If you value your life, you'll stop right there." She held up her hand. "It's you and me and no one else. I wonder why the universe just didn't make us twins like our dads."

Cora scrunched up her face. "Can I tell you something?"

"Um, of course." Rose laughed.

"For a while, I kind of—no, not kind of, I did feel like I

lived in your shadow and that's all anyone saw me as. I was just a stupid sidekick and super unimportant."

"What?"

"I know *you* didn't think that. But I thought everyone else did and they didn't like me because of it. Getting to know Dylan"—she began to smile, face lighting up like fireworks on the Fourth of July—"has kind of changed my mind. I think I felt like a shadow because I *believed* it. It was easier to stay unhappy than to put myself out there. Telling me to join the SEC was a really great idea."

Rose smiled too. "I definitely owed you one." She checked the time on her phone. "We have about an hour before Auntie Jackie will get here."

Unfortunately, her parents vetoed the Rose Should Skip School proposition. Their reasoning being something about needing to learn how to balance her responsibilities, as if she weren't on a strict deadline! Exceptions for dire circumstances should be considered!

And they said no to that too. She'd been so angry with them last night but regretted yelling at them *while* doing it. She'd never felt like that before. Thankfully she'd had another planner epiphany about them too. After getting dressed, she wrote them a letter saying she loved them and explained exactly why she was sorry. Then she taped it to their bathroom mirror so it would be the first thing they saw when they woke up.

"Armed and ready to be the lookout," Cora said.

"Okay. Here we go." Rose opened her textbook to a random page and unfocused her eyes. All her senses dulled, one by one. Trying to remember how the Connection felt was like walking through a darkened hall cut off from everything. She felt disoriented and weightless—what was up, what was down, where was left, right? If she didn't move, if she just curled into a ball, maybe it would find her.

That was ridiculous. Connections didn't work like that. It should have opened. She called for it, and it should have welcomed her. But it never did. Not even once so far.

Someone was saying her name. Every time she heard it, the dark hallway pulsed with light before fading just as quickly.

"Hey!"

Rose inhaled, blinking rapidly. She watched Cora remove one of her earbuds and look up too.

Samantha stood in front of them, one hand on her hip. "You know, if you're going to pretend to read, you should at least turn the page every few seconds to keep the facade going." She set their drinks down before walking away.

"You were supposed to be the lookout," Rose said to Cora, who shrugged.

"I figured it might be better if she came over here. Which she did. So."

"Why would you think that?"

"I don't know. It just came to me, and I went with it," Cora said. "How is she feeling?"

Rose started to answer but had to stop. She wasn't quite ready to admit how flawed their Connection was. "I'm going to try some charms. Better yet, I think I'll use an enchantment today."

"Which one are you thinking of?"

"She's blocking me out, so I think I need to figure out who she's willing to let in."

"Blocking you out?" Cora looked confused. "How?"

Rose reluctantly explained the issue—that Samantha could repel all of Rose's magical influence.

Cora said, "Oh, man. If that's what they gave you, what are they going to do to me?"

"Whatever it is, I know you'll crush it." Rose grinned, checking her phone again. Forty-five minutes left. She began to tap her fingers on her desk in a simple repetitive rhythm.

Rose didn't have time or the means to use a charm. Luckily, Auntie Jackie started teaching her how to use sonic enchantments. Whereas charms had to be tied to physical objects and could only affect one person at a time, enchantments used sound and could affect anyone in hearing distance.

If a Matchmaker wasn't careful or was inexperienced, their enchantment could go rogue, becoming an earworm.

Once that happened, it would begin skipping from person to person like a stone thrown at the perfect angle across a lake. The ripples would grow and grow until the Matchmaker found a way to stop it.

Rose wanted to keep her enchantment contained to the café so Samantha didn't get bombarded by every guest in the hotel. Auntie Jackie taught her a couple of advanced tricks to stay in control. Instead of enchanting the sound, she would have to enchant *the person* while they hear it.

She began drumming on the table, a fast and playful beat.

"Cora?"

"Ready," she said.

Auntie Jackie hammered it home that Rose was never, ever allowed to try enchanting people without Cora there to run interference. If the enchantment went rogue, Cora would have to run to each affected person. A Matchmaker's touch was the only way to snap someone out of it.

Rose set each person inside the café in her sights, sending a thrilling pulse of magic at them in time to her finger tapping and timed exhales. One by one they turned to Samantha, smiling.

Her *Gotta Tell You* enchantment wouldn't make them fall in love with Samantha, of course. All it did was swing the odds in favor of them being a little nicer to her, to talk to her, to ask about her day with a kind smile. If it worked the way

Rose hoped, eventually Samantha's customer service sheen would fade into something genuine for the right person.

Rose kept it up, not pausing or stopping. Every time a new person walked by their table, she compelled them too. She held it for as long as she could until finally a wave of dizziness washed over her. As she grabbed the table so she didn't fall out of her chair, her stomach roiled and her head began to throb with an instant headache.

"Are you okay?" Cora's concerned voice cut through Rose's sudden illness. "You look a little . . . sweaty."

"I feel sick all of a sudden." The vision in her left eye began to blur.

"Maybe we should go upstairs? So you can lie down? Or throw up in peace?"

"Good idea."

Cora had to help her stand up. Rose leaned on Cora as they made their way to the elevator together.

"I think I must have held the enchantment for too long. What time is it?"

When the elevator doors opened, a boy with blue hair exited as they went in. Something about him seemed familiar. Rose tried to remember where she'd seen him before. Maybe at check-in? She couldn't think. The huge headache blooming between her eyes demanded all her focus. She overdid it. She should have never tried to push herself and her magic that hard. As the door closed, she continued to watch Blue-Hair Boy walk directly to the café. Samantha immediately spotted him. Their Connection pulsed bright white like a flash of lightning and faded just as fast.

Rose's hands shot out to stop the elevator. "Who is that? We have to find out who that is!" She tried to take a step forward, and her traitorous knees gave out on her.

Luckily, Cora caught her before she hit the floor.

"I really think we need to go upstairs," she said, struggling to hold Rose up.

"We will, I promise. I just need to talk to him first."

"You need to rest," Cora said firmly. "How about this: we go upstairs, I put you to bed, and I'll come back down here and do everything in my power to find him, okay?"

"Do you promise?" Even Rose's sturdy shins began to feel like Jell-O. Walking was out of the question. "Samantha *reacted* to him. That can't be a coincidence."

"Cross my heart. I won't let you down." Cora pushed the penthouse button and jostled Rose to get a better grip on her. "Literally."

Once upstairs, Cora quickly got Rose into bed as promised. "I'll talk to your parents and Auntie Jackie. I don't think you can go to school like this."

Rose nodded and immediately regretted it. *"Ow."*

Cora frowned as she fussed with the bedding. "Why do you only have two pillows? The appropriate number is abundance."

"I'm exhausted," Rose said. "Lecture me later."

"Denied."

"Then go talk to him, please?"

"Right after I tuck you in." Cora draped a throw blanket over her cousin. Without another word, Cora slouched down to lie next to Rose. She inched in close enough for their heads to touch, forehead to temple, and closed her eyes.

"I know what you're doing," Rose said weakly.

Cora exhaled, opening her eyes. Sometimes it didn't even work. Sometimes the images would suddenly slam into her so hard she almost fell over. "You're not fine," she said softly. "You feel like a hurricane. Pain and confusion hiding behind sheeting rain. I felt like I was going to snap in half—"

"Don't tell me how I feel, okay?" Rose looked her cousin in the eye. She didn't want to know, didn't want to hear it. If completing this Singe meant faking it until she made it, then that's what she was going to do. "I don't care if you can see it. I'm fine. Positive vibes only."

Cora pressed her lips together as she nodded. "Okay. Well, if you ever decide you're not fine, I'm here for you."

"I know. Thanks," Rose said. "Now will you please go?"

"Be back as soon as I can." Cora sat up, rolling into a standing position. "Also, you really need a new bed. This thing feels like rock-hard stone."

A familiar sound filled the room, capturing their attention—the strike, crackle, and whoosh of a match catching fire and being blown out.

"Oh no," Cora said. "Oh no, no, no not now."

It appeared on Rose's desk, propped up by a box of tissues. Cora nearly face-planted in her rush to get it. She looked at Rose, who shared the dreadful feeling written all over her face. Not too long ago, Red Letters were exciting. She loved getting them, loved meeting her Kindlings, loved planning with Cora—love, love, love. They represented a chance to tap into who they were, who they were born to be. Now they were both wary. What near-impossible challenge would she have?

Cora held up the Red Letter with shaking hands, her name emblazoned on the front.

Attn: Coretta Marjorie Seville

Challenge in the First by Order of the Oracle Council

Rose said, "You have to open it. Just get it over with. No matter what it says, we got this."

DYLAN: Are you here yet?

D: At school, I mean.

D: I guess I'll just go to class then. Unless you're running late?

D: Did you stay home today?

D: Is everything okay? Amber said Rose didn't show up either.

## Chapter 12

Devastation.

It was the only word to describe the feeling when something you didn't even know you wanted was dangled in front of you until you realized you did want it and then it was brutally snatched away. Complete and utter devastation.

Dylan Matthew Jackson

and

Ariel Rita Lucille Meyer

It was a brand-new Band-Aid being ripped off a sensitive patch of skin. It was stepping on a rock and rolling your ankle until you fell, scraping your hands and knees in the process. It was brushing your hair and hitting an impossible knot threatening to pull that entire patch straight out of your scalp.

Dylan being Cora's Kindling hurt like that—harsh, sharp, and lingering.

"Are you *crying*?" Aunt Tanya hovered in the doorway, holding the doorknob in a death grip.

"I'm not crying. I'm sick." Cora sniffled to emphasize her point. "I don't feel good." She didn't want to lie, but she also didn't want to tell the whole truth. "Is Rose better?"

"She's getting there." Aunt Tanya hurried across the room and sat on the bed. She pressed a hand against Cora's forehead and then her cheeks. "You don't feel warm."

"I'm congested." And devastated.

"You certainly sound like it." Aunt Tanya looked concerned, eyebrows pulling together. She sighed once, looking uncomfortable. "About Dylan—"

"You're not allowed to help me."

Cora sniffled again, wiping her nose with her hand. She focused on her bedspread so her aunt couldn't read her face. Two sides of her life had collided and now everything was imploding. She just needed some time to figure everything out. To adjust. To let go.

*Why was this happening?!*

Aunt Tanya sighed again. "All right, well, I guess you're both staying home today. I have to go into the office, but Jackie is going to come by to check on you girls. Maybe bring you some soup."

After she left, Cora rolled over, curling into a ball. Crying took up a considerable amount of time. Hours had passed before the tightness in her skin, around her face, and the puffiness around her eyes began to feel unbearable. Her head hurt too—a headache that pulsated in one eye.

And yet, somehow, she still had the strength of will to get some water and medicine.

Her body felt sluggish. Sitting up was like trying to pull herself out of quicksand and took up the last dregs of her energy. This was how she would exist now. A gnarly tortoise. An exhausted sloth. She'd make it to the kitchen eventually.

Next to one of her pillows, her phone rang. The screen filled with a long number she didn't know but recognized as an international call.

Cora's heart chugged to an abrupt stop as she answered, voice barely more than a whisper. "Hello?"

"Cora?"

*"Mom?"*

"Hi, honey," her mom said. "I'm sorry I couldn't call sooner. I got your first message—"

"It's against the rules." Cora had to take deep gulping breaths to stay calm and not dissolve into incoherent babbling mush. "I know. It's okay."

"Well, I couldn't then, but it's fine now. I got special permission to give you a call," she said. "You know how *persuasive* I can be—nothing keeps me from my baby when she needs me, you hear me?" Her mom knew. She was with the Oracle Council after all. They must have told her firsthand how they planned to set up Cora. She continued, "I can't tell you what to do, but I can listen."

"Everything was horrible. I hated it here so much. I just wanted you and Dad to come back."

"I know."

"I didn't have anyone except Rose, but she has her own life, and I didn't fit in there." Cora sniffled. "And then I finally found someone interested in *me*. Not because I was Rose's cousin and she asked them to give me a chance, but because they liked *me*. And now that feels like it's all over. It's not fair."

"You're right," her mom said gently. "This is deeply and incredibly unfair. It's okay if you're not okay. You have the right to not be okay with this."

"What am I supposed to do? I don't want to fail, but I don't think I can do this."

"Oh, honey, I wish I had an answer for you. It's your challenge. You can take it on however you feel is best. If you want to walk away, you can. If you want to complete it, you can. Whatever you choose, as long as you stand by your decision, we'll stand with you."

## Chapter 13

From now until I ascend,
I promise to learn from my experiences.

Rose lay on her bed, her entire body aching. Muscles, joints—gosh, even her teeth. Her parents sat on either side of her.

"I feel awful. Please send help." Her voice sounded weird—muffled and a bit slurred.

"If you feel well enough to talk," her mom said, "would you mind explaining how you managed to nearly deplete your reserves?" She placed a damp, cool cloth across her forehead.

"I did *what*?"

"You're not sick, honey," her dad said, worry and sadness warping together in a disapproving tone that only a parent could deliver in a crushing blow. "You've been using too much magic. You always have been, actually. At the rate you were completing your Singes, we honestly thought it would be fine."

Her mom said, "Edward reported that you don't keep an inventory of your magic. Even though we knew you didn't, we assumed you still knew how. We shouldn't have done that. We should've made sure to teach you a long time ago."

Rose knew her magic was finite, that she could use it all if she wasn't careful. But at any given moment, she never knew how much she had—she just knew she had it. And now she didn't. "I used all of it? Really?"

"Very nearly. That's why you're in pain. Your body is going through withdrawal. Our magic becomes a part of us. Once we start using it, our bodies adapt and expect it to always be there, even if it's just a little bit."

Her dad said, "Think of it like your stomach being empty. If you wait too long to eat, your stomach starts to hurt. Same concept."

"We're going to give you some of our Singe energy to tide you over until you complete your challenge. This is a one-time deal. We won't be allowed to do it twice, so you'll have to ration what we give you carefully."

"*Ration?*" Rose asked.

The pain flared up again. She'd been trying to keep her eyes open, keep perfectly still, but they'd just dropped a bomb on her, and the shock wave forced her to move. She also began to feel embarrassed—cheeks heating up, tears pricking her eyes. Her parents had to give her magic as if she were a youngling. As if she weren't a Fledgling on the fast track to becoming a Flyer.

"You can do it. We know you can," her dad said. "Close your eyes. I'll walk you through how to create a way to check your inventory."

Rose did while continuing to be as still as possible.

Her dad continued, "It can look any way you choose—a jar, a shoebox, a closet, as big or as small as you want. The most important thing is it's somewhere safe and something you can hold in your mind."

She began to imagine a stone walkway leading to a small cottage surrounded by a field of wildflowers. Insects buzzed all around her. She smelled the babbling freshwater creek not too far away, watched the smoke pluming from the chimney. It was peaceful there. Quiet.

"Do you see it?"

"I do."

Her mom said, "We'll start on the count of three."

Shimmering maroon and golden ribbons of light drifted down from Rose's sky. They approached the front door and waited patiently for it to open. She continued watching from the field, and with a flick of her wrist, the ribbons found their way inside.

Sweet, cool relief washed over Rose, putting out the fire that had been burning her from the inside out. Her parents' magic restored her strength and her channel and her hope.

Rose opened her eyes and sat up, feeling better than she had in weeks. And immediately started sobbing. Her parents loved her. Really, truly *loved* her. Was this what a Singe was like? Overwhelming and all-consuming to the point where she wasn't sure where she would be without them?

Because her family *loved* her so much, it was almost too much.

Almost.


Too late to go to school and too late to try asking Samantha, Rose ended up at the front desk to get started.

"Bobby," she sang. "Hi."

Bobby had excellent front-desk energy. Angry customers were no match for his unflappable and charming smile. He knew all of Hotel Coeur's rules and regs, shortcuts, and never forgot a guest's face. He was the perfect person to help her. Rationing magic might end up being as hard as completing her Challenge in the First . . . but she wasn't out yet. She *could* do this.

"Miss Rose." He was typing faster than any person she'd ever seen and while looking at *her*. She could type without looking too, but talking to someone would totally distract her.

"I need a favor," she said. "I'm looking for a guest."

"Name?"

"I don't know."

"Room?"

"Don't know that either."

"Then what do you know?"

"He has blue hair."

"We live in San Francisco. Everyone has blue hair."

"We don't."

"I'm being facetious, sweetie."

Rose playfully stuck her tongue out at him and then smiled. "He's also young. Maybe your age?"

"That certainly narrows it down," he teased. "I'll see what I can do."

"Thank you so much. I'll be upstairs for the rest of the day. My cousin is sick, so I'm going to take care of her."

Bobby nodded. "I know where to find you when I find him."

When. Not if. Rose grinned. "You're the best."

"I'm aware of that." He grinned back. "Tell your parents to give me a raise while you're up there."

# Chapter 14

Unwilling to face the struggle ahead, Cora decided to stay home the next day too. Rose, recovered and ready, went to school like normal. She texted her throughout the day, trying to cheer her up.

**ROSE: Update—Samantha was off today BUT Bobby found Blue-Hair Boy. His name is Ryan Longo and get this, his family is set to check out after their art show wraps up, which just happens to be my Red Letter deadline. COINCIDENCE? I think not.**

**R: I think that's why I have a time limit and you don't. He physically won't be here much longer so I have to Singe them soon.**

**R: I'm 94% positive he's Samantha's match.**

**R: Are you still in bed? I love that for you.**

**R: Yes, I'm getting your homework and taking detailed notes**

during class. Don't even ask.

R: Dylan was extremely mopey at lunch. Pretty sure he misses
you.

R: Okay yeah he was worried enough to ask me if you were okay.
Maybe text him?

R: He's asking if you're okay with visitors coming to your sick
bed.

R: He wants to know if you like flowers.

R: Brace yourself. I'm telling you now so he can't surprise you.
He's planning to ask you ~something~ important.

R: . . . Your challenge is so messed up omg.


"Knock, knock."

Cora regretfully lifted her head from her pillow fort.
Auntie Jackie stood near her bed with a giant glass of
water. A single contemplative eyebrow slowly inched
upward toward her hairline. Cora had never seen her without makeup—darkened, shapely eyebrows, a mole dotted
on under an eye, thick fake eyelashes swooping like wings
every time she blinked her hazel eyes.

"Well, aren't you a sight," Auntie Jackie drawled. "Tanya
said you were sick. She didn't say lovesick."

"I'm not—"

"Don't try to lie to me, child. Broken hearts are my
specialty. Nobody is better than me when it comes to
Whirlwinds."

That much was true. Cora had grown up with stories about how Auntie Jackie had singlehandedly created a subset of Singes called Whirlwinds, which had to take place immediately after a heartbreak.

Ever heard a story of someone falling madly in love in under twenty-four hours? Or of someone being left at the altar only to find the One a handful of moments later? That was Auntie Jackie and her crew at work. It was the stuff of rom-coms in real life.

She held out the glass of water for Cora to take and sat down on the edge of the bed. "Name?"

Cora hesitated. "Dylan."

"And what did they do?"

"Nothing."

"*Mm-hmm.*"

"He didn't do anything." Cora shrugged. "Really."

"Then why this"—she waved her hand in Cora's direction—"production? Hmm? I can feel it," she said, cocking her head to the side. "Your strings are . . . discordant and knotted. Feels like conflict. Indecision. Not quite heartbreak, but it's around the corner."

Cora sat up, wiping her eyes to clear them and pay attention. "Wait . . . how? You can feel my heartstrings? I thought—"

Auntie Jackie scoffed, pinning Cora in place with an amused look. "Sensing strings is woven into the very fabric of our being. We are who we are. And some of us have abilities that others don't, which I'm sure *you* know all about."

Cora nodded in place of confirming specifics. Edward told her not to tell anyone else that she could see emotions and pathways, but odds were good Rose already spilled the secretive beans.

"We are who we are," Cora repeated. She was responsible for Dylan now as his Matchmaker. Thinking about him and the letter was like another Band-Aid being ripped off. She'd have to give him up before she'd even had a chance.

Auntie Jackie said, "There it is again. I can practically hear it, snapping and snarling in anguish. What happened?"

Cora considered her options. She hadn't even said the words out loud yet. Saying it could help her get used to the feel of them. Help her accept the truth. The Oracle Council expected her to facilitate Dylan's match.

"We met at school. He likes me. I like him too," she said quietly. "And now, he's my Kindling."

Auntie Jackie sucked in a breath through her teeth. "Those monsters," she growled. "I'd say I can't believe they'd do this to you, but that would be a lie. I'm sorry, dear."

"Me too." She felt so hollow inside, as if someone had reached in with an ice cream scoop and took everything out.

"Although," she said, and then paused to twirl a strand of hair around her finger. "There may still be a way around this. You're assuming his match will be a romantic pairing. There's no guarantee that it will be."

That was also true. Matchmaking never focused solely on romance. Love did not have boundaries, so neither did they. Whatever their Kindlings' hearts truly needed, Matchmakers were honor bound to create the match.

Cora said, "But he's still my Kindling. We're not supposed to be paired with people we're assigned to."

"The Oracle Council isn't omniscient." Auntie Jackie leaned forward, keeping her voice low. "Your Dylan wouldn't have been assigned a Matchmaker if he didn't need help in some way. But that might not have anything to do with what the two of you have. Sometimes they even create matches that will suit their needs to serve their 'greater good.'

"I can't get into specifics, but once, I had an assignment for an American politician that involved a love triangle. Let's just say when presented with the choice, he didn't exactly follow his heart because that meant he would have left his job. *They* needed him in office. He's happy, don't get me wrong, but I know for a fact that he still thinks about the one who got away and what could've been."

Cora didn't want to hope. She didn't want to believe. But it was too hard to resist reaching out and grabbing hold of Auntie Jackie's words with both hands.

"Really?"

She nodded. "I could help you. With this and . . . other things."

"Getting help is against—"

"The challenge rules are clear. You may not receive guardian help." Auntie Jackie pointed to herself. "*I* am not your guardian. You've barely scraped the surface of what a Matchmaker can *really* do. There's so much more to what we are that they don't want you to know. I could show you. I *can* help you."

Cora had shoved her Red Letter in a drawer across the room so she wouldn't have to look at it. So, she could pretend it didn't exist, even though she could still smell the roses. She sniffled again. "Help me how?"

CORA: Hi.

DYLAN: How are you??

D: I've been kind of worried out of my mind ahaha.

C: If I told a lie would you let it slide?

D: Depends on the lie.

C: I'm fine.

D: Are you sick?

C: I'll be at school tomorrow.

D: Okay.

D: Hey, would it be okay if I called you?

## Chapter 15

*From now until I ascend,
I promise to listen to my matchmaking elders.*

"I need to do more reconnaissance on Ryan. There has to be something that will make him interesting to her. Are you listening?"

Cora grumbled, "No." She was partially buried under a mountain of blankets and pillows. Only a hand, a leg, and the top portion of her face were visible.

Rose, on the other hand, was completely dressed and ready. She would've loved to jump into bed and sleep the day away with Cora, but neither of them had that luxury right now. "Do you think you're up for school today?"

"Mm-hmm."

"It's going to be a *get ready in five minutes* day, isn't it?"

"Mm-hmm."

Rose kissed her cousin's (sweaty) forehead. "I'll call you when Auntie Jackie's here. Samantha is scheduled today, and if she's there, I should be too."

"Mm-hmm."

"Good talk. Go team."

In the lobby, Rose didn't see the person getting off the elevator next to hers. She slammed into him, dropping her bag.

Blue-Hair Boy. Ryan. Talk about kismet. Luck was clearly back on her side.

"Sorry," he said, immediately picking up her bag and handing it to her. "Rose, right? Your parents own this place? I always see you running around."

"That's me," Rose said, and decided to add, "Are you a morning person too?"

"I'm not," he said, with grave seriousness. "Pretty sure my brain is still sleeping." But he was dressed in jeans and a clean T-shirt. And his hair appeared to be brushed.

"Sleepwalking, then?"

"Not quite." He gave her a slight smile.

Rose narrowed her eyes. "Then what are you doing up?"

"Doughnuts mostly." He looked over her shoulder, straight to the café where Samantha's top bun bobbed up and down over the counter as she wiped the glass clean, getting rid of all the streaks.

"You know we sell them all day, right?" she said.

"Oh. That's cool," he said. "They taste better in the

morning, and besides, it's kind of a habit now."

"Right. I'm sure that sudden habit has nothing to do with our resident surly redhead."

"Uhhh." He laughed awkwardly and cleared his throat. "Am I that obvious?"

"No," she admitted kindly. "Just an educated guess."

"Yeah," he said, rubbing the back of his head. "So, uniform. School." He gestured toward her.

Rose nodded. "How are you here by the way? Are you homeschooled or something?"

"No. How old do you think I am?" he asked.

Rose raised an eyebrow. His social media profiles didn't list his age, but Samantha was twenty-one, so he must have been around that age too. "You really want me to answer that?" She couldn't resist teasing him.

"Nope." He laughed. "I travel with my parents a lot, so I have online college classes."

"Where's their art show again? Your parents, I mean. My dad was advertising it to guests, but I didn't catch the venue name."

"All week at the Golding Rush Art Center. You should stop by. It's pretty cool, in my completely unbiased opinion."

"Are you an artist too?"

"Not like my parents, but yeah, I guess. I like to think so anyway."

They reached the café, and only one person was ahead of them in line.

"I'm going to flex some nepotism privilege and hop behind the counter. See you."

"Yeah. Bye."

This time, instead of trying to surreptitiously make hot chocolate, she continued on to the small kitchen, where Samantha was placing two sandwiches into the industrial convection oven.

"What do you want?" she snapped.

"Are you working alone again?"

"Why do you care?" Samantha began to wipe crumbs from the surrounding counter.

"I was thinking maybe I could help," she said. "There's a bit of a line, and I didn't see anyone else on shift. I don't have to leave for school for a few more hours."

Samantha paused in mid-wipe, slowly turning her head to look at Rose. Even her eyebrow took its sweet time raising into a question mark. "You want to help me?"

"I'm helping my parents, and by extension I'm also helping you." A little white lie wouldn't hurt anything. Since Rose couldn't use magic on Samantha, she decided to give the old-fashioned way a try. With only a week to go, and a whole lot to lose on the line, this was exactly what Cora would do. And it was way better than burning out on magic again.

The beginnings of a new plan began to whisper to her. All she had to do was figure out a way to get a certain doughnut dealer to agree to it.

Samantha regarded her for a moment. "Aprons are by the freezer."

Rose ended up staying for a full two hours. She was sure Samantha steeped herself nightly in jerk-flavored tea, but she worked hard. And she was an attentive coworker. She didn't yell at Rose if she made a mistake. She took her time explaining how the oven worked. If Rose got over-whelmed with front-counter orders, Samantha appeared like a supportive phantom to help her. No questions asked. She smiled at guests, even calling some of them by name.

It was . . . unexpected. "You're a lot nicer than I thought," Rose said. They were sitting in the back together, Samantha showing her how to count and prepare the register till for the next worker coming in soon.

Samantha barked out a laugh. "No. I'm really not."

"Seemed like it," she muttered with a shrug.

"I need this job. It pays surprisingly well for food service, and I get benefits. I'll smile until my lips crack and start to bleed as long as I get paid."

"Oh."

"Not everyone has rich parents and gets to live in a swanky hotel, princess. Some of us have it a lot harder."

Rose's face flushed in embarrassment. "I didn't mean—"

"I know you didn't," Samantha said, returning to the count. "You're not so bad yourself when you stop being an overbearing try-hard."

"Try-hard?"

"Everything about you screams you think you're better than everyone else. I mean, if that's how you feel, cool, but don't get mad when everyone you think is beneath you doesn't want to worship the ground you walk on."

"I don't think that. I just have a lot of confidence in myself. Why is that a bad thing?"

Samantha shrugged. "You tell me."

"Don't you care if people don't like you?" she asked instead.

"Nope."

"How come?"

Samantha put the till count in a plastic bag and sealed it. She sat back in her chair, thinking. "Being liked by strangers means something to you. I don't feel that way. I have myself. I have my people. That's enough for me."

"People? You mean like your family?" Rose asked hopefully.

"I don't have a family," she said, looking Rose in the eye. "Not like you have. No parents. No cousin. No one."

"Sorry," she said, kicking herself. "I shouldn't have asked."

Rose had never felt so awkward with a Kindling before.

Under normal circumstances, she'd be able to sense the kinds of things they could talk about that would enhance their Connection in a safe and fun way. Trying to coax information about Samantha *out of* Samantha, piece by hard-earned piece with no help felt like torture. Embarrassing, clumsy old-fashioned torture.

"If I didn't want to talk about it, I wouldn't have," Samantha said. "I have people I care about and who care about me. It's enough."

A thought sprang to life in Rose's mind: *What would it take for her to see Ryan as one of her people?*

"Do you like art?"

"Why?" Samantha asked, visibly confused by the question.

"There's this art show I want to see, but my parents can't take me and Cora."

Samantha scoffed. "You help me out on one shift and suddenly you think we're friends?"

"Of course not," Rose said, thinking quickly. "I can pay you." She cheesed then, all teeth and cheery desperation.

"Been awhile since I babysat a kid," she said with a teasing laugh. "Depends on what time. I have a gig tonight."

"Gig? Like music?"

"Yeah," Samantha said, beaming suddenly. Her whole face changed, lighting up with joy and purpose. Rose had *never* seen her look like that. Bright and infectious, it made her want to smile too. "I play guitar in my band, Expired Makeup. We have a deal with this club to play a couple of nights per week. It's kind of like a Vegas residency sort of thing except *way* cheaper." She laughed, sincere and happy.

"That's really cool," Rose said. "We don't want to go too late. Right after we get home from school would be great. Speaking of, I should go. Gotta make sure my cousin actually woke up and got dressed."

"All right. Just let me know," Samantha said. "Thanks for your help today. It was real chill of you."

Rose smiled at her, waving goodbye as she walked into the front. She checked her phone, and—surprise, surprise—Cora was already in the parking garage with Auntie Jackie.

Inside the car, Cora looked half-dead. She was awake and breathing, but the zombie vibes were high.

"Can you even use Scyther right now?" Rose teased. "It looks like all of your focus is going toward keeping your eyes open. And that's not even working."

"I'll watch your next swim meet." Cora threatened Rose with an adorably bleary-eyed gaze. "Is cheering allowed? Go! Swim! Win! Or something? Don't make me find a way to embarrass you with my unconditional love and support."

"You wouldn't dare."

"Haven't you heard?" Her voice began to slip into a

mumble. "I have mastermind energy." Cora's eyes drifted closed, and she began to slump forward.

Auntie Jackie leaned on her horn.

*"Oh my god."* Cora placed a hand on her chest, taking deep breaths.

"Wake up," Auntie Jackie said tersely.

"Crying is exhausting! I'm tired!" Cora shouted. "I'm here, aren't I? That should be enough!"

"Here and still asleep," Auntie Jackie said. "Wake up, child. Listen to me carefully so you don't mess up. The Oracle Council is watching you closely now—especially since your mom intervened for that phone call. They're very curious to see where your loyalty lies: yourself or your duty. To get what you want, which I'm assuming is both, you must work around their radar."

"Me and my mom call that the gray area," Rose said. "You're following the rules, clear as day, but you're also sneaking around at night right under their noses."

Cora paused, staring at her cousin. "Do you know what a mixed metaphor is?"

"Focus," Auntie Jackie snapped. "There's no denying you're not as gifted as your cousin."

"Thanks for the reminder."

"But that doesn't mean you don't have potential in other areas. Your issue is matchmaking is a work of heart and magic. You don't believe in yourself—because you can't, because you're too cerebral and stuck in your own head. It both helps and hinders you, canceling it out into mediocrity."

"Wow, you give spectacular compliments, you know that?"

"I'm saying you need to pick one. Instead of trying to balance them both, choose the side that suits you best," Auntie Jackie said. "The only issue is, of course, that no Matchmaker would ever tell you to do that because it's never been done before. There is a first time for everything, and I wouldn't be surprised if that becomes your second challenge, so you might as well start working on it now."

Cora asked, "What does any of that have to do with Dylan?"

"Nothing," she said. "But it was something you needed to hear."

Rose tried not to smile, because Cora was *never* in her shadow, not to her. Cora saw people's emotions just by touching them, Scyther actually obeyed her commands, and her planning powers were nearly flawless. Different didn't mean she was a failure. She just needed a separate set of matchmaking standards. Logic and understanding. Control and skill. To Rose, her cousin shone brighter than anyone else.

"I thought you were going to help me," Cora said.

"I *am* helping you." Auntie Jackie side-eyed Rose, who beamed with encouragement to balance out Cora's contrary attitude. "You need to test your compatibility with Dylan to get a definitive answer."

Cora asked, "We can do that?"

"There's no rule against it. Just some ethics and gray area."

Cora said, "Not against the rules doesn't mean that it's allowed though. Is there something else I could research? Just to be sure?"

"Start with the entry on heartstrings. Read between the lines—it never says you can't look at yourself *while* assessing your Kindling's heartstrings, which is something you'll have to do *anyway*. Two birds. One very gray stone."

"Then what?"

"*Aht aht.* One step at a time to start. I know how hard that will be for you."

Cora scoffed, turning to gaze out the window. She slipped on a pair of giant dark sunglasses.

Auntie Jackie turned to Rose. "And you?"

"Me? What about me?"

"Your Singe, peanut. What have you been doing?"

"Oh, it's going." Absolutely no one else could know her parents had to donate magic to her. She was partially down, but nowhere near close to out. She'd pass her challenge, have her own magic again, make her parents proud, *and* beat Julien—all in one Singe. "I think it's going to come together really soon."

Auntie Jackie pulled up to the front of the school and put the car in park. "Good. I'd expect nothing less."

Chapter 16

Months ago, before Dylan and San Francisco and moving, Cora had been assigned a practice Flyer Matchmaker exam. She'd been so nervous that she threw up all over her Kindling's expensive shoes while trying to establish the Connection. The disappointment didn't stop there—her parents ended up having to take her assignment and finish it for her.

She completed plenty of supervised Singes since, found her groove and her way, but the super-important ones? They always decimated her stomach. Disaster, thy name was Cora.

"I shouldn't have eaten this morning."

"That was one time," Rose said dismissively. "One epically hilarious time."

They stood near the stairwell, just outside of the cafeteria. "What if I mess it up again? I'll open my mouth to say his name, and my partially digested oatmeal will come out instead."

It was one thing to projectile vomit on a teacher from a rival school during a football game, but to do the same to Dylan? He might never forgive her.

Rose snorted. "I'm sorry. It's not funny . . . but it is."

"It's kind of funny," Cora admitted. She swallowed hard. *Don't even think about it*, she commanded her stomach. Her nerves always seemed to get the best of her. She hated it so much but didn't know how to make it stop. Making an official Connection with Dylan would be difficult enough without the added pressure of her previous gastrointestinal failure.

Cora had been dreaming about being a fully inducted Matchmaker-in-arms since she was five years old.

Her Singe setups took place in coffee shops and malls and theme parks and office buildings because she figured at some point she'd have to cosplay as a business professional to reach her Kindling. She always wore the best outfits, which felt more like disguises—fluttering dresses, cool-girl jeans and leather jackets, thick-rimmed glasses and berets, and jewelry borrowed from her mom's closet.

She was never shy. She never doubted herself.

Most important, she could feel each moment. How overjoyed she'd be to meet them. How much her face would hurt because she wouldn't be able to stop smiling.

How *tired* she'd feel from staying up too late researching potential matches if she ended up with one Kindling instead of two. How dedicated she'd be to finding what their heart wanted. Ready to do her best, to make them proud, to stop at nothing until the job was done.

Maybe her dreams had been too naive. But was she wrong for wanting them?

Was she being punished for it?

Dylan rounded the corner. He spotted them immediately.

Rose took Cora's hand and gave her an encouraging squeeze. "Game time. You got this," she said, before deserting her.

"Hey," Dylan said, smiling brightly. He seemed so happy to see her it physically hurt.

She tried to smile for him. "Hey."

"So, you're alive."

"Only just so."

His smile switched to concern instantly. "Are you feeling better?"

"Not really," she said with a shrug.

"Do your eyes hurt or something? Is that why you're wearing sunglasses inside?"

"Yeah. Helps with the migraine. You know, light sensitivity." She pushed them up her nose. "Anyway, did you have plans for lunch today?"

"Nothing out of the ordinary. Why? What's up?"

"Wanna eat outside? I think the smells in the cafeteria might tip my sensitive stomach over the edge."

"Sure. Just us, or is Rose coming back?" He craned his head to the left to look inside the cafeteria.

"Just us?" she said, suddenly feeling shy. "Is that okay?"

"More than okay." He grinned.

Outside, they sat under one of the smaller trees near the parking lot. The weather felt surprisingly springy for an autumn day. A calm sun and the kind of chill in the air that let you get away with only wearing a sweater but was warm enough to keep the grass dry.

"Hey, do you know someone named Ariel?" Cora asked.

Dylan handed her a soda from his backpack.

"What's this for?" she asked.

"Whenever I'm sick, my mom makes me drink ginger ale to help settle my stomach. The cafeteria only has Sprite, so I brought this from home."

"Thanks." Cora stared at the can in her hands, knowing that if she blinked, she'd start crying, and if she started crying, he'd ask what was wrong, and she would cry even harder because this was the new worst day of her life. And then she'd feel bad for making him worry and cry some more.

Dear lord, she'd just been emotionally compromised by a can of soda. The day could certainly only go up from there.

He looped his arms around his knees. "So."

"So."

"I was wondering if you'd heard about a dance coming up. A weird masquerade ball or something?"

"Oh, I think I might have," Cora said, playing along. "Isn't it super exclusive though? Only certain people can attend."

"Funny story, I actually have tickets." He cleared his throat. "I was wondering if maybe you wanted to go? Together. Officially. I mean we'll both be working," he said, dropping the pretense, "but I figured we could still have fun before the mystery starts."

Cora opened her mouth, but no sound came out. *Oh no,* she was staring at him. She could *feel* herself staring and not moving and not talking and *ruining* everything.

She should say no.

She was *supposed* to say no until she knew for sure what he needed as her Kindling.

Her palms felt clammy. She sat the soda down and rubbed them on her plaid skirt, swallowing hard as she tried to find her voice.

Dylan continued to wait for her answer. His dark brown

eyes were as patient and unassuming as ever.

Cora felt like she couldn't breathe. Her chest ached—she inhaled but the air wouldn't go down, stopping in her throat. Her eyes felt wet, but they burned so badly. She felt wound up tight as a hot coil, ready to melt, ready to stop existing and reform as something else. Why was the Oracle Council making her do this? They hadn't had a chance to really *be* anything yet. She wanted to explore more places in San Francisco with him, take more pictures, and hold his hand. There was so much more she wanted to talk to him about. She wanted to learn everything about him, wanted to listen to him laugh and meet all his favorite people.

She didn't want to do this. It wasn't fair at all.

"I would love to go to the dance with you." Cora wiped the single tear that managed to fall. "Dylan Matthew Jackson." She breathed, exhaling the sinergy she had retrieved in advance and reaching for him with her mind. She imagined a delicate ribbon wrapping around his heart and binding them together. Luminous green mist began to swirl in his irises.

Cora didn't want to know Dylan's secrets because of a Connection. She wanted him to tell her, on his own, because he wanted to, because he trusted her. This felt wrong, like a precious moment being stolen from them.

She wanted to be his friend, not his Matchmaker.

But it was her job.

His heartstrings told her about its desires in fluttering images and sensations. What he wanted felt like down feathers tickling her arm and like warm sunlight on cold snow—vivid and dazzling and conflicted. His thoughts sharpened and focused around, the image of a tall girl with blond wavy hair. And a name: Stacey. Part of him was fixated on her. There was something else, smaller but just as powerful. No, not small. *New*. Whatever it was, it hadn't had the time to settle and flourish like the image of the blond girl.

Cora shivered, skin tingling with promise like the first taste of cotton candy. When she found his eyes again, an electric shock hit her heart.

"Cool." He laughed. "I was surprisingly worried you'd say no for some reason." He smiled at her like she was his favorite person in the whole world. And then, he held her hand.

Once a Connection was established, Matchmakers could tap into their Kindlings' heartstrings whenever they wanted, and Cora held on to Dylan's with care. She kept them close to her own, where they'd be safest.

But now she had to perform Singe step three:

compatibility test. Dylan's story began with two people: Ariel and Stacey Mondragon.

Unlike Matchmakers, regular human heartstrings were devoid of color until they connected with someone else. Some were special—regular humans with black strings had learned to connect with themselves, which helped them connect with others. That didn't mean they wouldn't be a Kindling candidate someday. They were just less likely to need the help.

The worst connection was white. Two sets of strings together and no response whatsoever? An automatic failure.

Rose waved Cora forward from her hiding place farther down the hall. "That's her," she whispered. They traded places so Cora could peek around the corner to spy on the two-toned blonde wearing a cat-ear headband.

"I can't believe she's a candidate." Rose frowned. "She's been horrible since fourth grade, once her boobs grew in. I didn't think that actually happened outside of movies."

"She might not be," Cora whispered back. Fixation was a common obstacle to work around. Kindlings didn't always know what was best for them. "Okay. I'm gonna do the test." She reached behind her—Rose took her hand and gave it a firm squeeze.

"You got this."

Cora placed a hand over her heart. With her mind, she

gently tugged on Dylan's heartstrings inside of her. *Go to Stacey, please*, she asked them. Some candidates shivered when contact was made. Others laughed like they were being tickled. For Cora, it felt pleasantly weird, like a flurry of dandelion seeds swirling around inside of her.

Stacey, however, began to rub her chest, wincing a little. "Oh god. I think I have heartburn."

Her friends laughed. When Dylan's strings touched hers, the reaction was instant—a solid gray of indifference. *Yikes*. That was a definite no.

It must have been an old lingering crush that Dylan still wasn't over. Stacey was his past, not his future. Cora breathed a sigh of relief and let go. His heartstrings practically ran to her, eager to be back in their hiding place.

"It's not her," she said with a smile.

"Oh, thank *god*." Rose gave her a tight hug. "Now, about this Ariel business. I found her."

"Really?"

"Amber knows all; she sees all," Rose said. "And she says Ariel is a loner with a reputation for never talking to anyone if she can avoid it. She's also super into photography. If you want to find her, she's usually in the old darkroom on campus B after school. But you can't go today."

"Why not?"

"There's a couple of art show tickets with our names on

them waiting to be claimed," Rose said, smiling. "I *might* have come up with a little plan. Be my backup?"

"Oh, yeah. Sure. What's the plan?"

"Samantha is going to babysit us."

"I'm sorry, I don't think I heard you right. *What?*"

DYLAN: I'm really happy I got to see you today and I'm glad you're feeling better.

CORA: Me too. Both counts.

D: Can I call you tonight?

C: Maybe. I have to do some family stuff and then catch up on the homework I missed.

D: We could do our homework together.

D: I promise I won't be too distracting.

C: Liesssss.

D: Okay fine I promise to keep distractions to the bare minimum. Once per thirty minutes?

Chapter 17

At the gallery, they handed their tickets to the doorman and headed inside. The art was advertised as an immersive experience, each room designed to elicit a different emotion and reaction. The recommended "absorption" period was ninety minutes.

"All right, children," Samantha said. "Let's go be sponges."

Rose didn't have time for that because her countdown clock was practically screeching at her. "Actually, we have to find someone first," she said.

"I'm only being paid to watch the two of you. I'm charging extra if there's a third rugrat," Samantha said.

Cora nearly cracked a smile with her snort. "Rugrat."

"You don't have to watch him too. He's a friend," Rose said, and stopped a man carrying a drink tray. "Excuse me, where's the reception area?"

He smiled at her, friendly and amused. "You don't want to walk through?"

Rose said, "Not on your life. Where is it?"

He laughed and pointed to a darkened hallway on their right.

"Thanks."

At the end of the hall was another gallery, the typical kind. Frames hung on white walls, there were a few sculptures here and there, as well as benches for people to sit, and harsh lighting that showed *everything*.

"Wow am I glad I wore sunglasses," Cora said. "Thanks for inviting me, by the way."

"It was either you or my parents were gonna start following me around secret service–style, which, apparently, is *not* considered helping," Rose said, scanning the room. She honestly expected them to show up anyway.

"You know, for thirty seconds I felt special." Cora looked at the floor. "Come on, ground. Open up and take me. Save me from this embarrassment."

If anything, Cora's despair had caused her humor to go into overdrive. She started wearing dark sunglasses *anytime* she had to leave her room to hide how bad her eyes looked from crying so much. If someone asked about the glasses, she had a different response at the ready.

*Eye infection.*

*It's the only defense I have. I'm at war with the sun and she's out for my retinas.*

*I burst all the blood vessels in my eyes. Every last one. Do you wanna see?*

*Getting my pirate's license and I refuse to wear an eye patch, so glasses it is.*

*Snuck into a makeup warehouse and had a little too much fun with the waterproof products. Don't tell the police.*

"There he is," Rose whispered, pointing to him. "You should try the *Call Me Maybe* enchantment. It'll be good practice."

"This is your night. Don't pull me into it. I got my own problems." Cora rolled her shoulders anyway, taking a moment to focus. She began to hum, low and monotone. "Ryan," she hush-whispered in a reverent tone and clapped her hands once.

The sound wave—a near invisible iridescent green—headed straight for him. Rose watched as it avoided everyone, twisting through their legs, winding around their waists, and soaring over their heads so they wouldn't hear it. Five seconds later, Ryan looked straight at her as if Cora had yelled at him from all the way across the room.

*"Nice."* Rose high-fived a stunned Cora. She *nailed* it.

"I can't believe that worked. And on my first try? Twice in a row?"

"Twice?"

"What are you two whispering about?" Samantha asked.

"Nothing!" Rose said, all innocence. "We found our friend."

They maneuvered through the crowd until they reached him. He stood next to two people who had to be his parents. His features favored both equally—his mom's thick hair and eye shape, his dad's fair skin color and height. He also looked bored, like he wasn't listening to whatever the adults were talking about.

"Hey, Ryan," Rose said. "This is my cousin, Cora."

"Oh, hey. Nice glasses."

"Oh, hey. Thanks."

"And," Rose said, standing a little taller, "this is Samantha. She gave us a ride."

Ryan reacted immediately, stiffening with a surprised expression. His gaze darted to Rose, who wiggled her eyebrows at him and threw in a wink for good measure.

"I know you," Samantha said, cool as ice. She crossed her arms and unleashed a sly half smirk. "Vanilla latte and cruller doughnuts. To go."

He smirked back. "Good memory."

"You ordered the same thing every day this week."

"That I did." Ryan began to blush. It spread furiously right across his cheeks.

"It's fine," Samantha said. "Most people usually do. Makes my life easy."

"Well, um." Ryan cleared his throat. "Since you're here, how about a guided tour?"

Cora said, "Sure," as Rose said, "Is any of your art here? I wanna see that."

"Changed my mind," Cora said. "I would also like to see your art."

Ryan began to flush again, this time from the neck up. "Oh. Uh. Well. Um."

"You *do* have some here. I knew it!" Rose exclaimed.

"It's not *mine* exactly," he said, keeping his voice low. "I had an idea for one of the rooms. My dad and I collaborated on it. That's all."

"Still wanna see it," Cora and Rose said in unison.

Cora whispered, "Jinx." They grinned at each other.

Samantha stared at them for a beat, eyes narrowed. "I didn't realize how creepy you two are until just now. You should hold on to that." She turned to Ryan. "For the record, I would also like to see your art."

"Guess I'm outvoted, then," he said with a laugh. "This way."

Ryan reluctantly led them back toward the entrance. He made them linger in each room, explaining the theme and symbolism. Rose knew he was stalling for all that he was worth. She kept time—he got five minutes per room before she started hustling him forward. Finally, they reached room number 4. His first grand work of art.

As he talked about his creation, his face lit up just like Samantha's did when she talked about her band. If she weren't a Matchmaker, Rose was sure she would've missed it. The feeling behind the smiles affected her almost identically. That same brightness, that same willingness to join in. That similarity couldn't be a coincidence.

"This seems like a good match," Cora whispered. "Body language between them is on point. She's even *smiling*. How are the heartstrings?"

"Still can't see them. I was so sure once they had a chance to talk that Samantha would let me. I don't understand why she's still resisting."

"There has to be something else you can try."

Rose began to chew on her thumbnail. No strings, no Singe. Unless . . . "Maybe I could try an instant-Singe?"

People had it wrong. Love at first sight wasn't a real thing, but Singe at first sight could definitely happen with the right Matchmaker at the helm.

Cora's eyes widened in surprise. "That's *really* advanced, Rose."

She wasn't wrong.

But what other choice did Rose have? She had to do *something*.

"Desperate times, blah, blah, blah. Did you bring Scyther?"

Cora paused, lips pressed together as she thought. She

patted her book bag to check and then shook her head.

"Shoot. I think I remember how to do it, but I want to check first."

"Rose. That takes a lot of magic. You almost passed out from holding an enchantment too long." Cora's gaze suddenly unfocused. Her arms fell slack at her sides.

Rose recognized what was happening immediately.

Cora was visualizing—some strategic options must have come to her. Her eyes began to move left and right slowly as if she were watching a snake slither back and forth across the room, tracking it very carefully. Suddenly, she exhaled. Her eyes filled with panic and concern. "An instant-Singe might use up all your remaining magic *and* knock you unconscious."

"Is that the *only* outcome? What if I don't get another shot like this? *Look at them*."

"Hey," Samantha shouted, forcing them both to look at her. "If either of you are thinking about running off, I will find you, I will catch you, and you will regret it. Got it?"

Rose rolled her eyes. "We're not going anywhere. We're just talking."

"I know what plotting looks like when I see it."

Rose waited for Samantha to turn her attention back to Ryan before saying, "Okay. I'm going to try it anyway. I have to. I think I just make a pathway and hold it open."

"Hold it open for how long?"

"I don't know!" Rose threw her hands in the air out of exasperation. "I don't remember!"

"Listen to me, please." Cora held Rose by the forearms, so they had to face each other. "I'm not saying it's not the right plan, but if you don't know exactly how it works, I don't think you should risk it."

"He's leaving soon. If I don't risk it now, I don't know if I'll have another chance." Thoughts of failing and the avalanche of consequences that would follow stung like an angry, insistent wasp living its best life all over her body because, make no mistake, that species' sole reason for existence was to hurt people.

"There's still time for us to set something up again," Cora said. "We'll check the guidebooks, figure out another way to get them together and try the instant-Singe. I'll back you up all the way. But we're not prepared to do this right now. We're just not."

Rose blew out a frustrated huff of air. She felt in her heart that an instant-Singe was the right move and firmly believed she had to do it right then. But that could've been the desperation talking, influencing and daring her to risk it all.

Because if Cora didn't *think* she could do it . . . she was probably right. Logic was her specialty. She wouldn't have lied about what she'd seen.

"Fine," Rose said reluctantly. It hurt worse to concede

defeat than she thought it would, manifesting as a low persistent ache deep in her stomach that also felt like regret. "You win."

Cora shook her head. "It's not about winning. It's about being safe and making a plan. You got this far with barely any Connection. You're literally doing the impossible, Rose. Don't mess up now by getting impatient and being reckless."

Rose regarded her cousin, really seeing her in that moment, wise beyond her years, almost as if she were possessed. "Auntie Jackie was right," she said quietly. "You are too cerebral. You don't understand how this feels for me at all. It's not just about me failing myself. It's about me failing Samantha too. She told me she doesn't have any family, but she's supposed to have him. It's my responsibility to make that happen."

Afterward, Ryan and Samantha didn't even exchange phone numbers. It took all of Rose's strength to not glare at Cora the entire ride home.

DYLAN: Home yet?

CORA: Stayed late after school for a thing.

D: Really? You should have told me. I would've stayed too.

C: I know. That's why I didn't.

D: ???

C: A girl's gotta have her secrets.

D: Secrets from me? About me??

C: Stop being so intuitive. It's weird ahaha.

C: It's a surprise. Let me surprise you please.

D: Oh good. I have a surprise for you too what a coincidence.

## Chapter 18

From now until I ascend,
I promise to always be true to my talent.

After school on Monday, Cora thought it'd be better to wait outside the darkroom for Ariel. She ended up sitting on a short set of steps near the front door. Typically, she would spend her time studying Scyther but wasn't in the mood. She felt too sad to do anything.

Rose refused to talk to her over the weekend. At all. About anything. She wouldn't even say good morning at breakfast.

The truth was she did have Scyther with her at the art gallery. She never went anywhere without it. At first, Cora just had a feeling it wouldn't go well . . . so she lied. She felt terrible about it, but if she had looked up how to create an instant-Singe, she knew Rose absolutely would have tried it. But then her suspicions were confirmed—there was no way Rose would have been successful at the art gallery.

All she did was tell the truth. Now Rose blamed Cora for ruining *everything*.

She didn't mean to make Rose upset, but she knew she did the right thing. Being sad was just the price she had to pay for that.

Her "Emo Music for My Hurt Feelings" playlist had officially hit thirty songs and counting.

Cora wondered when she'd feel like herself again. When the pain wasn't being rubbed in her face like lemon juice on a cut, she mostly felt numb. It was like someone hit the mute button on her entire existence. There, but also not.

Dylan's heartstrings were a double-edged sword. Holding them, knowing they were there, made her feel like she'd been wrapped in sunshine. But then she remembered why she had them in the first place and slipped away into nothingness again.

She didn't like touching her Connection with him for the same reason. That reminded her: Auntie Jackie's advice. Cora was supposed to look up those entries. "Looks like we're doing this now after all," she said to Scyther as she pulled it out of her bag.

It'd been a while since she looked up something so basic. The day she got her guidebook, the first thing she did was memorize the Singe Steps because it took *so long* to retrieve them. Looking back, two days wasn't that bad. She'd seen Rose struggle for a week trying to get one question answered.

The second thing she did was give it the name Scyther because it asked her to. It listed the Singe Steps and wrote:

Coretta Marjorie Seville, I do not wish to be referred to as "my book." I formally request that you give me a proper name, posthaste.

Cora set her intentions and asked: *I'd like to see the standard entry for "heartstrings" cross-referenced with "compatibility."* She had to be specific. Otherwise, Scyther would give her its spicy version.

Heartstrings are the primary determinant for desire after establishing a connection with a Kindling. They are essential to determining compatibility with other Kindlings and/or potential matches.

That seemed incredibly straightforward. Cora had no idea what Auntie Jackie expected her to interpret from that. She wasn't a Kindling. She wasn't a potential match. "Scyther, can a Matchmaker be compatible with their Kindling?"

Yes.

Cora's eyes widened. She did not expect that. Keeping her voice low, as if the Oracle Council could somehow hear her, she asked, "Is there an entry explaining why?"

Compatibility comes in many forms. It is the Matchmaker's responsibility to determine which kind would be best for their Kindling through the evaluation of heartstring results.

See also: heartstring color theory.

Now turn the page.

She did.

I can see what you are thinking. I do not recommend it.

Wow. That was *also* incredibly straightforward.

Cora was distracted, in the middle of considering her options when her phone rang. She answered without screening the call first. "Hello?"

"Hello, hi, Cora? This is Edward from the Oracle Council."

She slammed Scyther shut so hard it hurt her hand. Were they *watching* her?

"Oh, hi!" She tried to fix her face, hoping she didn't

look as guilty as she felt. Just when she thought her day couldn't get any worse, now she had to worry about council surveillance.

"I'm afraid I have to apologize. I had every intention of returning to do this in person. However, that's no longer possible. Would you mind updating me on your progress?"

"Sure." Cora stared off into the distance. She had to keep it short, sweet, and factual. Nothing extra. "I received my Red Letter. One of my Kindlings is a friend of mine, so I established their Connection first. I have their heartstrings. I'm waiting to have my Matchmaker meet-cute with my second Kindling right now, actually."

*"Wonderful."* He sounded surprised. "Very good. I will look forward to seeing your results."

"Okay." She dropped her guilty gaze to her feet.

"One last thing: I collected enough data to make a conclusion. The council feels confident in the results without the need for further testing. Additionally, I spoke to your parents, and they agree as well. Tell me, do you know what a diviner is?"

"No."

"I suspected as much." The sound of ruffling papers took over the call for a few seconds. "Diviners are a rare subset of Matchmakers who can see the unseen. Your mother suspected you might be one, which is why she taught you reflective rumination. She was delighted to hear that she was right."

Rose might have been onto something with naming people her nemesis. Cora began to grind her teeth. She wanted to tell her parents about it herself. Now, the Oracle Council had snatched that away from her too.

Edward continued, "You've even met a diviner before. Jackie can inexplicably see the heartstrings of any person without a connection. Most are like her, with only one ability. You have *two*. Do you understand how special that is?"

At that moment, Cora was still too sad to care. Maybe she could get excited about it later, after checking with Scyther or talking to her mom. Right then, constantly worrying about Rose and thinking about Dylan over-whelmed everything else. She didn't have any more room. She felt like a plant trapped in a too-small pot. "From late bloomer to leech to diviner. Look at me go," she said dryly. "Thanks for letting me know."

The darkroom's doors opened, and suddenly a streak of dark blue flew into the air. Literally flew because Ariel tripped over her feet and went soaring palms first down the short steps. Loose papers scattered everywhere.

Cora watched the whole thing happen like it was in slow motion. "I have to go!" She hung up on Edward and rushed to Ariel's side. "Oh my god, are you okay?"

Ariel Rita Lucille Meyer looked exactly like her picture in last school year's yearbook. She had wild, curly black hair and dark eyes that were too far apart on her bronze-colored face. Her tiny nose made her full lips look unbalanced. So odd and yet, her face just *worked* somehow. She was the kind of pretty that made people stop and do a double take. She'd also scraped her hands and knees raw. Grimacing in pain, she said, "Um, my stuff."

"I'm on it." Cora sprang into action collecting every sheet of paper she could. The wind wasn't blowing, thankfully, so she was able to gather most of them. A few had fallen into a puddle and were already ruined.

Ariel managed to stand up, but Cora had to help her put the papers back in her bag because her hands were bleeding.

"Thanks." Ariel took a step and it turned into a limp.

"Is your foot okay?"

"I don't see any bones sticking out. Gonna consider that a win," she joked. Her first full sentence sounded light and airy like a bird.

"Do you want to go to the nurse?"

"No, I'm already late." She closed her eyes and let out a deep breath. A single tear escaped her right eye, and she wiped it away with the back of her hand. She tried to take a step with her left foot and had to stop. "No, no," she whispered. "This isn't happening."

"Do you need help getting to where you're going? I have time."

"Um, my bike is over there?" she asked hopefully, gesturing to the bike rack closest to the parking lot.

"Yeah, of course," Cora said. "You can lean on me."

Cora's arm brushed Ariel's waist—she gasped in surprise. Dylan's heartstrings reached out on their own like heat-seeking missiles. They intertwined with Ariel's, resulting in an automatic scarlet-red bloom. Their strings desperately clung to each other, burning hot like a fire. Deep melodic chords began to sound in her head, the crescendo crashing like waves onto the beach.

A match. A serious, actual match. Cora didn't even *need* to establish a Connection with Ariel. This was a rare, real deal.

"I keep a first aid kit in my basket. My dad is going to be psyched when I tell him I finally used it."

"Being prepared is important," Cora said, voice hollow.

"Sorry about this," she said. "I'm Ariel."

"Cora. And don't worry about it. Just doing my job."

"Job?"

"Being a good Samaritan. It's our civic duty to take care of each other, you know."

"Socialism for the win?"

Cora laughed. And hated herself for it.

Ariel retrieved her tiny kit from the black basket attached

to the handlebars. The bike was also black, with a single silver stripe and whitewall tires. Cora helped her clean her cuts and place Band-Aids on the larger scrapes to help with the bleeding. They used a small roll of gauze to wrap the palms of her hands.

"Thank you," Ariel said again. "You really didn't have to do all this."

"I told you it's fine. Do you think you'll be okay to pedal?" Cora asked. "My auntie picks me up—we could give you a ride?"

"Oh, no, that's too much. I'll be okay." To prove it, she swung her hurt leg over the bike and straddled it. Cora eyed her skeptically but didn't say anything. "Um, do you like lasagna?"

"Lasagna?" Cora asked.

"Yeah. When my dad finds out I fell, I'm going to tell him you helped me, and he won't leave me alone until I invite you over for dinner to properly say thank you. He's an entire ordeal." She rolled her eyes affectionately.

"I don't dislike lasagna."

"Are you free tomorrow?"

"Sure."

"Cool. I'll give you my number, then."

Amber must have had bad intel. Loners who liked to avoid people didn't just invite strangers to dinner or give out their phone numbers. They didn't have a Connection.

Ariel was being nice just to be nice.

Cora managed to smile. "Cool, indeed."


Later that night, Cora sat on her bed with her laptop open. She'd found Ariel's social media profiles.

Ariel must have wanted to be a photographer. Her public profiles were full of animal portraits and scenic shots. She seemed to enjoy capturing bridges and traffic at night. Some shots had been edited—a beautiful field of sunflowers had been transformed into a lifelike rainbow, bursting with colors as if they grew out of the ground like that. At school, she was in the photography club and on the volleyball team. She made the honor roll every year.

In private (Cora had sent her follow requests that were approved in what had to be record time), she complained about school and her parents' divorce and her therapist. She loved posting song lyrics and yelling in all caps about how powerful they were. Selfies were rare. Videos even rarer. She wanted to travel the world, taking pictures of famous landmarks because they hadn't been captured through her eyes yet. Her posts didn't have many likes. She didn't seem to have many friends either.

But what surprised Cora most was her latest update. Ariel had taken a picture of her bandaged hand. The caption read: *Met an angel named Cora today. I think my life is going to change.* She stared at the post, wanting to delete it, wanting to keep it, wanting to get to know Ariel, wanting to keep Dylan to herself, wanting to—

Cora's phone beeped.

**D: Can I call you?**
**C: Call? On the phone?? Again???**
**C: . . . Yes.**

Dylan called her in seconds. "Hello."

"Hello." She pushed her research away.

"Important question—I *have* to know the answer to this."

Cora sat up straight with worry. "Okay."

"What is the best deep-space terror movie and why is it *Alien*?"

"Wrong. It's *Pandorum*."

"No, why would you say that?! I thought I could trust you."

Cora allowed herself to laugh, to breathe and relax.

They ended up talking for hours and hours and hours until she was in bed, in the dark listening to Dylan tell her about the time he got stuck at the top of a Ferris wheel at the county fair. She felt unreal, soft and dreamy. Everything as infinite as it was temporary. If they stayed right there, together, then it would never end.

Cora stared at the ceiling, and her vision began to blur.

His gentle heartstrings began to twirl and dance on the ceiling like ribbons fluttering in the wind. They sparkled and shined with envious internal light.

And then, she placed a hand over her heart.

Her own strings were more hesitant. Afraid to reach out. Afraid to try. She trusted that comforting, familiar shade of vibrant green to know best.

Their strings latched on to each other, spiraling and weaving together into intricate braids.

Was this their Connection? Because they were Kindling and Matchmaker?

In places, the braids began to shift colors, blooming into a soft red for romance, a delicate yellow for loyalty, a cerulean blue for intense friendship—and a blushing pink for love.

They *were* meant to be.

A Matchmaker Connection couldn't possibly contain that much possibility.

They were meant to be *everything* to each other.

"Cora?" Dylan asked sleepily. "Are you falling asleep on me?"

"No," she said quietly as she tucked their heartstrings away. "You'll hear me snoring when that happens."

"You snore?"

"Like a magical piglet with asthma."

He laughed. "Most girls wouldn't admit to that."

"Why not? It's not like I can hear it, so it doesn't bother me. My mom recorded me once to prove some long-suffering parental point," she said. "Wait, hold on. Did you just 'not like other girls' me?"

"I didn't say that."

"But you implied it, and I totally fell for it." She rolled over and yawned, feeling content for the first time in days. "That thing really is insidious. Hits you before you know what happened."

"Okay, wait. I didn't though." He paused. "Oh crap, maybe I did. Wow. That *is* insidious. I'm sorry."

"It's okay," she said. "Fun fact: I'm actually not like other girls. They don't seem to like me."

"Not true." He laughed, quick and amused. "Next you're gonna say you get along with guys better. Let's go full cliché."

"Let's not. It's just easier talking to *you*," she said, feeling safe enough to finally tell him the truth. "It's different with girls. I want them to like me. I get nervous and clammy. I'm scared they won't get my humor, or think I'm weird, so I just don't say anything."

"But anyone could think that about you."

"That's very reassuring," she deadpanned. "It's just different with them. I don't know how to explain it."

"Hmm." He was quiet for a several heartbeats. "So you want to be not like other girls while with the other girls?"

"Yes. That's exactly it. Nail. Hit. Head." She thought of Christine and Amber. She thought of Ariel and how quickly she wanted to be her friend even though she was Dylan's match and would take him from her. "They're all so pretty and radiant. They're like Barbies, no, Bratz dolls. Definitely Bratz. And I'm like a Muppet compared to them. A sarcastic, flailing Muppet."

"You don't flail."

She waited. "And?"

"Oh no, you're definitely a Muppet. Nail. Hit. Head."

Cora cackled into her pillow. "Shut up."

"What?" His voice dipped low and soft. "I like Muppets. I like *everything* about Muppets. They're my favorite."

*Oh no.*

Chapter

19

Rose had woken up frustrated, cranky, and her mood refused to let up throughout the entire day. A dense fog of *Why is life so exhausting?* had settled around her. Wading through it seemed impossible because her muscles felt tense, her movements stiff.

"Good afternoon, peanut."

"*Hmm,*" Rose grunted in reply as she put on her seat belt.

"Excuse me?"

She amended her grunt to a grumbly, "Good afternoon."

"That's more like it," Auntie Jackie said. "Where's Cora?"

"Connecting with Kindling number two." Rose slouched down in her seat, crossing her arms. "She goes to our school."

"You still giving her the silent treatment?"

Rose refused to answer. She didn't feel like getting lectured again. Her mom yelled at her. Her dad tried to reason with her. Even Christine *and* Amber thought she was overreacting—she kept the matchmaking specifics to a minimum and they *still* took Cora's side. Why was no one on her side? Why couldn't they just let her be *mad*? She'd talk to Cora when she was good and ready. Maybe.

Auntie Jackie waved her hand at Rose and her bad mood, bracelets clinking together musically around her wrist. "What's all this?"

"Not really feeling the whole *I exist and people can perceive me* thing today."

Auntie Jackie's scoff turned into a laugh. "You're too young to be that existential, peanut." She shook her head. "Try to save it for when you turn twenty-five. Existential dread hits different during a quarter-life crisis. Trust me."

Rose smiled, a bit of sunlight breaking through her fog. That was the amazing thing about Auntie Jackie—she took her seriously. Always believed and never talked down to her like she knew better *because* she was older.

"Still no Singe?"

"Nope. The stench of failure continues to smother me."

"Stop being so dramatic."

"I *am* the drama," Rose whispered.

"Apparently."

"I worked in the café with Samantha this morning. When I innocently asked her what she thought about Ryan, she accused me of trying to set her up with him. She laughed in my face and told me to stay in my lane. Me. ME. We *invented* that lane. I may *never* recover."

Auntie Jackie tried to muffle her laugher with her hand. "For what it's worth, it's good to fail occasionally. It keeps you humble."

"I don't want to be humble," she admitted, glancing at Auntie Jackie from the corner of eye. "What's the point of that?"

If it had been her parents, they would have looked concerned and proceeded to lecture her for at least an hour. Auntie Jackie, however, smiled.

"I don't know. Truthfully, I've never seen the value in it, but it is an expectation worth acknowledging in public. It will make people like you, make you relatable," Auntie Jackie said. "When you're as powerful as you are, others will create a place solely to try to put you in it. Standing *next to* their expectations gives them the illusion of control until you're ready to do your own thing. Understand?"

Rose nodded. Her challenge could've been over by now if she just trusted her instincts. "*Julien* called me yesterday and *forced* me to know that not only has he completed his challenge but also knew from a 'good source,' aka his *mommy*, that the Oracle Council had expected me to be done already. He was *surprised* I was still working on it. He had the *nerve* to sound disappointed."

"That sounds like him," she muttered. "Tell me why your Singe hasn't happened yet."

Rose told her the entire story, starting at the beginning to the horrible Connection and ending with the night at the art show gallery. She had one shot and she blew it spectacularly because she let her cousin talk her out of it. Matchmaking at its core was a risky business. Matchmakers had to learn how to trust their hearts and take a leap of faith. She'd been ready to put it all on the line, but Cora convinced her to second-guess herself. Cora made her doubt.

"To be fair," Auntie Jackie began, "you were both right. The instant-Singe is actually a good call. I'm impressed you thought of it." She tapped her chin. "I think you can do it, but you wouldn't have been able to pull it off at the art show because you have to know exactly what you're doing. It's too precise of a magic to fake your way through that. It'll backfire faster than an old car and *really* smother you."

After Samantha had dropped them off at home, Rose immediately researched how to create an instant-Singe. The entire thing hinged on circumventing Singe step four: Conduit, which could only be used when Kindlings were compatible. There had to be chemistry and compatibility.

If a Matchmaker tried to use one without doing the work, literally nothing would happen. It'd be a complete waste of time and magic.

An instant-Singe created a magical bridge between two hearts, regardless of chemistry, heartstrings compatibility, or if a closed heart was involved—it had the power to ignore *everything* else. The magic took hold when the Kindlings, or a Kindling and their prospective match, looked into each other's eyes. It was just like that old saying "the eyes are the windows to the soul." Coincidentally, eyes also had some influence over hearts.

"When you perform the instant-Singe, you have to make sure you *believe* in what you're doing. That it's truly the *only* path for those two hearts. And you must visualize the bridge down to the smallest detail. It must be perfect. Flawless," Auntie Jackie said. "Do you *know* what can happen if it doesn't work?"

Rose nodded. Because the bridge was so powerful, if it backfired, that magic still had to go *somewhere*. Instead of connecting their hearts, it would do the exact opposite— they would hate each other on sight.

"And you understand that's a very real possibility? I've seen it happen more times than not. I believe in you, but it could honestly go either way."

"I do."

"Good. Don't ever let doubt diminish what you know

to be true. You have a gift the likes of which we haven't seen in generations. It must be nurtured and cultivated properly. I know it. Your parents know it. And the Oracle Council knows it. You, my peanut, are destined for greatness."

"I might not get another chance to prove it. Ryan is leaving soon and—"

"*Aht, aht.* I don't want to hear it. Do not doubt. You have to believe in your purpose, and it will match you."

Rose nodded and took a deep breath. Auntie Jackie was right. As long as she still had time, there was still a chance.

A chance was all she needed.

# Chapter 20

Death had finally come for Cora Seville.

She never thought she'd go out this way. Ungracefully bent over with her hands on her knees because she couldn't catch her breath. "That—should be— illegal," she said in between wheezes. "*That* is a murder hill."

Ariel laughed. "It's not *that* bad."

"My lungs disagree with you." Cora looked back down the steep slope. "You really walk up this thing every day? While pushing a bike?!"

"Yeah." She laughed again. "I guess I'm just used to it. Come on."

Ariel lived in one of the multicolored houses at the very top of the gigantically steep murder hill. Three levels including the garage, it had been painted the metallic blue and green of peacock feathers and trimmed in rich browns and plums. She led the way up the steep pink stairs to the front door and entered a code on the keypad attached to the wrought iron gate. It unlocked with an audible *click* a few seconds later.

All the curtains in the house had been pulled back to let sunlight fill the large entryway. Ariel didn't linger— after taking their shoes off, they walked through a back hallway, passed a bathroom painted an unbelievable lime green color, and ended up in the kitchen. "Just going to get some snacks," Ariel said. "My dad won't be home for another thirty minutes or so. He said he'll start cooking dinner as soon as he gets in."

Everything was polished and perfectly clean. In the far corner, a door stood open. Cora headed toward it, peeking her head inside to find a small landing with a connected set of stairs.

"The garage and the den are down there," Ariel said, holding a couple of snack-size bags of chips and sodas. "My room's this way."

They walked up a short flight of steps and made a quick right. Ariel's room was on the left-hand side. Cora expected the walls to be covered in photographs and prints, and she was not disappointed. There wasn't a single stretch of wall left bare. She'd even begun filling up the ceiling.

"How long did this take?" She pointed to the rainbow gradient of polaroid pictures on the back of her door.

"Taking all the pictures? About six months. It only took a couple of hours to put them up," she said, and then pointed to a small pastel yellow armchair, while she sat in her desk chair. "You can sit if you want."

Cora sat, sinking into the plush velvet. Ariel's room felt lived-in, loved and cozy. Fuzzy pink carpets, a bedding set with a proper pillow ratio that made Cora proud, moon phase and star constellation hanging sets, a laptop covered in stickers and a desk covered in nicks and scratches. It even had a height measure on the window frame—a new line for every birthday as she got taller.

Cora's room back home felt like this, at least she hoped it did. In Hotel Coeur, she was as much a guest as someone who had to check in when they arrived.

Ariel asked, "What do you like to do?"

"Not much," Cora said. "Hang out with my cousin mostly."

"You're not like a painter or anything like that?"

Cora snorted. "What about me says 'painter' to you?"

"I don't know." Ariel shrugged with a smile. "Nothing, I guess. What about hobbies? Sports? Games?"

What a weird line of questioning. Cora concentrated for a second while pretending to accidentally brush Ariel's arm to check for any emotions that wanted to be seen. "Sorry." As she chewed on her bottom lip, glimpses of a dry thunderstorm over a desert appeared in her mind.

There was something slippery about it—a blink-and-you-miss-it kind of playful vibe.

Small talk was boring, and Ariel didn't do boring ever. She'd rather make it a game. *Can she catch on? Will she notice? What can we turn this into?*

Cora decided to play along. "I'm on the School Engagement Committee. Vice chair, in charge of the upperclassman dance. It's not a lot of work for me though, since I'm kind of in charge."

"Oh." Ariel sounded less than impressed.

"Other than that, I only really have one thing I do in my spare time, and I can't talk about it." She'd make it interesting all right.

"How come?"

"Top secret family business."

"I won't tell anyone. Obviously."

"That's what everyone says until I tell them what it is," Cora said. "Either they don't believe me or they tell anyone who will listen." In reality, she'd never told anyone she was a Matchmaker.

"Are you guys vampires?"

Random, but okay. Cora said, "Nope."

Ariel narrowed her eyes like a wannabe investigative journalist. "Once, I heard a rumor that your cousin was royalty. Are you a princess?"

"I'm not *not* a princess. If I have a country or province

that recognizes my sovereignty is a different story."

Ariel laughed—another glimpse of lightning. "Okay. Okay. Um . . . werewolf?"

"Ew."

"What's wrong with werewolves?"

"What's right with them? Don't insult me like that."

"Are you a paranormal creature of any kind?"

"Define paranormal."

Ariel regarded her closely, slightly spinning in her desk chair. "An entity with any supernatural ability that normal humans don't have."

"Dang," Cora whispered.

Ariel laughed again, and so did Cora, despite herself. She'd been wanting this. She'd missed talking to her girlfriends about stupid things and playing silly games. Ariel seemed so serious, but she had a great sense of humor and a wonderful laugh. Why did she have to be a match for Dylan too?

"Am I close?" Ariel asked.

"Not specifically. I'm very talented when it comes to a very prolific part of life, and I have abilities because of it," Cora said cryptically. "And that's all I'm going to say. Hmm."

"Aww, come on! Give me a hint. A good hint. You don't have to tell me if I'm wrong, just confirm when I'm right."

"You'll never guess," Cora teased. "Not in a million love-filled years."

A voice called out from down the hall. "Girls? Where are you? I got Korean fried chicken for dinner. Hope that's okay! Cora, if you're a vegetarian I can also make a Mean Green Bean Casserole from Outer Space."

"A Mean Green Bean Casserole from Outer Space?" Cora asked, voice low. "What is that?"

Ariel groaned like only an embarrassed kid could when their parents strayed too far into Definitely Weird territory. She covered her face with her hands. "He promised."

Cora started laughing. "I can't wait to hear what the lasagna is called."

## Chapter 21

From now until I ascend, if I must fail,
I will do so with honor and grace.

Ryan was leaving the next day, and Rose had a splitting headache. Straight down the middle of her head like in a cartoon.

She wanted to yell every swear word she'd ever learned, in creative and nonsensical combinations until she felt better again. Tears stung the back of her eyes, and she gritted her teeth.

After her bedroom window seat that faced the sunrise, the rooftop was Rose's favorite spot in Hotel Coeur. She sat near the edge, right in front of the giant sign—glowing bright red and gold in a fabulous script. Down below, the streets were filled with honking cars, yellow taxis, and people traveling to wherever they needed to go.

The sun had almost dipped below the horizon. The city lights would begin twinkling to life soon. A black ocean full of stars on the land. Way up on the roof, the wind felt rougher, freer. She shivered against it but held steady.

Matchmakers were Kingmakers, the original influencers. Beguiling royalty blessed by the universe, heralded by gods, and foretold by prophets. Her heritage ran so deep in her blood, in her being, she had never once questioned who she'd be without it.

Rose couldn't just show up at Samantha's apartment with Ryan. The tenuous modicum of trust they'd built would crumble in an instant. If it were a box, she'd have to stamp FRAGILE on the side and pray a UPS driver (Samantha) didn't punt it like a football at a front door. Rose tried calling her to see if she could fill a nonexistent emergency shift for double pay (that her parents agreed to) but the call went straight to voice mail.

It was over. Everything was ruined.

Rose didn't even turn around when she heard the rooftop door open. She knew it could only be Cora anyway. And it was.

"His parents opted for the latest checkout we could give because they're not planning on leaving the area yet," Cora said, sitting next to her. "Ryan's dad made a dinner reservation at the hotel steakhouse for seven p.m. And I found out they have an overnight flight, so they're not leaving for the airport until ten p.m."

That was Cora's peace offering—research. Rose decided

to take it. "Doesn't matter. I don't know where Samantha is. I've been trying to reach her all afternoon." She tossed her phone back and forth between her hands. "How's Ariel?"

"Good, probably. I'm going to her house tomorrow for dinner again," Cora said.

"That'll make it three nights in a row. Wow. Things are getting pretty serious," Rose joked.

"I think she wants to be my friend." Cora laughed. "She doesn't really have any either."

"Do you like her enough to be friends for real? I mean, once she's not your Kindling?"

"Yeah. That's part of the reason why I don't want to make a Connection with her. I think I'm going to try it your way and stick to one Kindling. I don't know if I can handle having Ariel's heartstrings too. I'm kind of scared it might kill me."

"And Auntie Jackie says I'm dramatic." Rose snickered.

Cora bumped their shoulders together. "I'm really sorry about the art gallery. I should have just followed your lead."

"It's okay," Rose said.

"You were right. I wasn't thinking of Samantha at all. Even with Dylan, I'm trying to put him first, but I can't stop thinking about myself too—how I can make it work so I can be happy. It's not supposed to be about me. It's not supposed to be about Matchmakers period."

"'Matchmakers don't exist without their Kindlings,'" Rose said, quoting their guidebooks.

Cora gave her way too much credit. This entire time she'd been so focused on herself—on losing to Julien, betraying her reputation, and not being able to take her Flyer exam early. And then all those things started happening, *plus* she used up all her magic. It hurt something horrible, but really, she'd been just fine through it all because she had the support from her family, who loved her so, so much.

Arguing with Cora at the art gallery was the wake-up call she needed to realize the truth. Failing wasn't the worst thing that could happen to her. It was the worst thing that could happen to *Samantha*. Rose was the one shot she had at finding the perfect match she needed right now at this point in her life, and she failed her.

How dare she call herself a Wunderkind, the best of her generation, when she'd been nothing but selfish the whole time.

"Anyway, I shouldn't have interfered, and I'm sorry."

Rose exhaled a sigh, checking her phone for the tenth time in a single minute. "Auntie Jackie said we were both right. I think maybe I have a little too much heart and it makes me reckless sometimes. It makes me think I'm better and stronger than I really am. I think that's why we work so well together. We're opposites. We have what the other doesn't."

Cora laughed lightly, grinning. "I thought the same thing. Maybe it's because our dads are twins. They got split in half, so they passed on, like, halfsie Matchmaker genes or something."

"Huh," Rose said. "I have always wondered how they managed to get our birthdays exactly a month a part. Do you think it's possible—" Her phone chimed loud enough to make her jump and give her heart a violent restart. She'd forgotten she turned the volume all the way up. "Hello?"

"Hey, brat. What do you want?"

"Samantha! Hi!" She looked at Cora with wide eyes. Meanwhile, her cousin started slapping her arm. "Well, I, um, was hoping you could help me out again. Me and Cora wanted to go to this fun ballet thing but there aren't any BART or bus stops nearby. We'll pay you, of course, if you could give us a ride?"

Samantha laughed. "Are you really that desperate to hang out with me again?"

"You have no idea," Rose said honestly.

The line was silent for a moment. "When is it?"

"Tonight?"

"I can't. I have a show," Samantha said. "Remember the one I told you about?"

Rose nearly dropped the phone. "Oh, right! I'm sorry, I didn't know which nights you performed. Which club is it again?"

"Slim's on Eleventh. Why?"

"Oh, no reason. I'll let you go, then."

"I'll take you to the ballet thing though," Samantha added quickly. "Just not tonight."

"Maybe next week sometime?" Rose squeezed her eyes closed. Her heart was beating against her rib cage like a stampede of horses.

"Sure. Just let me know. Bye."

"Bye." Rose hung up and then promptly screamed with her entire body—flailing her arms, kicking her legs and shaking her head. "OH MY GOD!"

"What?" Cora demanded. "What did she say?"

Rose's heartstrings were three seconds away from vibrating out of her body. "Samantha's band has a show tonight. All we have to do is convince Ryan to ditch his family. This could work. This could really, really work." She jumped to her feet, running for the door.

Cora kept pace, right on her heels as the they descended the short staircase and booked it for the elevator. "If your parents buy the tickets and drive us, would that be considered helping?"

"It won't be if we don't tell them. We'll be vague, tell them they can't ask questions, and beg for everything we're worth," Rose said, almost out of breath. "If the Oracle Council has a problem with that, I don't care. This Singe is going to be the Hail Mary to end all eleventh-hour Hail Marys. It's for Samantha, not them."

"I'll get your parents. You get Ryan," Cora said, getting off at the penthouse floor.

Ryan was on the seventh floor, room 702. She had no idea if he was there, but it seemed like the place to try first before she ran around the lobby screaming his name. Desperate times, desperate measures, and she had amazing lung power.

Luckily, he answered shortly after she knocked.

"Rose." He sounded suspicious. "Hi."

"Hi. So. Question: Do you like Samantha?" Nuance, what's that?

"Um, uhhh, I don't really know her. I'd like to though. Wait, why are you asking?"

"She has a show tonight. She's in this really awesome band called Expired Makeup, and my family has tickets. I thought you might want to come. You know, since she came to your show, you can go to hers."

Ryan's gaze dropped to his feet, and he shook his head. "I don't think that's a good idea." He laughed lightly, as if he were trying to hide his disappointment.

"Really? Because I think it's a great idea. In fact, it may be the greatest idea I've ever had in my entire life."

"Look, you seem like a nice kid, and I know you guys are tight or whatever, but I don't think you're helping her out. She's not interested in me the way that I am in her, if that makes sense?"

"Did she say that? That we're tight, like she likes me? Never mind." Rose shook her head, waving that thought away. She had to focus—Ryan needed to be at that show. "And how do you know she's not interested in the same way?"

"It's pretty obvious."

"Did she say that?"

"No."

"Did you ask for her number?"

"No."

"Then how do you know?"

"Because I do." Ryan scoffed. "Why am I even explaining this? Why do you care? And, how old *are* you anyway?"

*Ugh*, this would be so much easier if she could just give him a charm! But Rose needed the little bit of magic she had left for the instant-Singe. How was she supposed to do this without magic? *Hail Mary*, she thought. *Just go for it.* End of the line.

Rose steeled herself and asked, "Do you believe in guardian angels?"

"What?"

"The tooth fairy?"

"Okay. I'm going to go. It was nice to meet you, Rose. Stay weird." He moved to go back into his room.

"Wait!" Rose slammed her hand against the door. She spoke in one long breath. "I care because I'm a Matchmaker and I've been assigned to help Samantha and she doesn't know it yet, but she has her heart set on you, and I've almost used up all of my magic trying to get her to trust me and it didn't work so now I'm breaking like a bajillion rules by telling you the truth because I can't create a charm to get you to go to the club but I know you want to be there too so I need you to trust me when I say that she *does* like you and that all I'm trying to do is make her happy. *Please.*"

Ryan blinked in surprise . . . and started laughing.

Turns out Rose's parents, who were smart enough to put two and two together and wise enough to keep the answer to themselves, had no problem with a spontaneous family outing to support Hotel Coeur's most beloved barista.

The main floor of Slim's was packed, but there was an upper balcony with tables and chairs. Her parents and Cora decided to sit up there to watch the show. Rose dragged Ryan over to the stage, as close as she could get to the front. "You stand right here. Do not move." They ended up just off to the side on the left because the crowd packed themselves in tight like a can of sardines.

"Why?"

"Because I said so! Don't you trust me?"

He laughed, shaking his head. "No."

"Well, you should," she said. "Rose always knows best."

"So, what exactly is a Matchmaker?"

"Me. My family. It's what we do. There are millions of us all over the world."

"Right."

She knew he didn't believe her, but that didn't matter. It worked. He was there.

He asked, "And you can all use magic?"

"They say you can't be one without it. I'm not so sure anymore."

"Ah, right. Because you used yours up." He smiled, soft and amused. "You really care about her, huh?"

Rose made eye contact with him. "With my entire matchmaking heart."

The radio music cut out. Rose's nerves were so far on the edge, they were ready to jump off the cliff. She stood closer to Ryan, taking quiet, calming breaths. The room faded away until all that remained were him, her, and a cranky barista about to find her person.

Rose visualized a purple wooden bridge straight out of a fairy tale starting where Ryan stood. She dotted it with flowers, music notes, and funky geometric shapes, being sure to hold it securely with her mind.

The curtain pulled back swiftly. Samantha faced the drummer, who began to count down, "One! Two! One two three four!"

Their first song kicked in, a catchy drumbeat with synth layered on top. Samantha began strumming, walking backward toward the mic. She must have counted the steps beforehand because when she turned around, she reached the mic *right* at the moment she began singing. Even Rose blinked in surprise when her sweet but strong melodic voice began to fill the room.

Samantha said she played guitar. She never said *anything* about being able to belt like a young Whitney Houston. Rose couldn't help but like Samantha's song. It was about feeling heartbroken because all she wanted was for someone to stay, but they wouldn't. So she decided to move on and never look back. An undeniable melancholic bop.

*This is a crime*, Rose thought. Why could everyone sing *except* her?

Misery aside, she managed to keep her focus and keep the bridge ready for Samantha to walk across. Every second that passed, more borrowed magic streamed out of her, and she sensed her inventory dwindling. She remembered what would come next: feeling dizzy, the headaches, her Jell-O knees—but she had to hold on. She would *not* let go of this bridge.

Everyone around her began to dance and crowd in closer to the stage.

*Come on, come on! Look at him,* she thought.

But it was obvious Samantha had already been consumed by her love for performing.

By the time Expired Makeup played their last song, Rose was utterly exhausted. Again. Every time she thought about giving up, her brain said: *What if Samantha looks over here and I miss my chance?* And so, she waited, and waited, and waited.

"Oh, thank god," Rose said after they finished.

She shouted, "Samantha! Hey!" while waving one arm. Holding on to Ryan, she pushed anyone in her way out of it, maneuvering around everyone else to reach the front.

"That was amazing," Ryan said. "Wasn't she amazing? I almost don't believe how good she is."

"It's a miracle," Rose said through her teeth.

Her mouth had never felt so dry in her life. All the moisture! Gone!

She shouted, "Samantha!"

Finally, Samantha looked up. She'd been putting her guitar in a case and began to smile as she walked toward them. "Hey, Princess Brat. What are you doing here?"

"We came to see you play." Rose made sure she had a

firm hold on the bridge she'd created between them and pushed Ryan forward.

"You were amazing." He let loose the dopiest, most lovestruck smile Rose had ever seen.

But Samantha looked toward the back of the club. "Is that your cousin up there? And your *parents*? Did you bring your whole family?"

Rose turned her head to look. Cora was jumping up and down, waving at them and chanting Samantha's name. Her parents had a bit more restraint. But not much. She shook her head as she turned back around. "Of course I did."

"Why?"

"I told you," Rose said. "We wanted to see your show. They had no idea you were in a band, and when I told them, they bought tickets, so here we are."

"Oh," Samantha said, slightly dazed.

Their Connection, Kindling to Matchmaker, suddenly exploded between them. Rose *gasped* from the force of it. The darkened hallway she'd been trapped in before blazed with light. Samantha's heartstrings, as tender and delicate as gossamer, flowed into Rose, and she finally understood everything. Her Kindling had been waiting for someone who cared about her—really cared about her and her well-being—to let them in. By being there at the club, by bringing everyone she loved to see Samantha, Rose had proven herself worthy.

And she didn't waste a single second.

Hearts finally open, Ryan and Samantha connected on the instant-Singe bridge, igniting with warmth and potential. It surrounded them, wrapping them up in a smoldering cocoon of magic. Almost instantly, Rose felt the Connection beginning to burn away, unable to withstand the surge of energy the Singe had generated as it poured into her. Her thank-you gift with a promise to pay it forward.

Connection severed, Rose smiled at her former Kindling and her match. Their Singe was finally complete. Relieved and ridiculously pleased with herself, Rose practically skipped back to her family.

CORA: Did you get the picture?

DYLAN: Yep. Ordering my tie as we speak.

C: Perfect.

C: Everything's going to be perfect.

D: It already was.

C: I'm not sure what you're aiming for with that.

D: You've been secretive lately. I was trying it out.

C: I'm not being secretive. I've just been busy.

D: Too busy to text me back?

C: There's this thing I have to do. It's really important.

D: I get it.

C: It'll be over soon, I promise.

D: Okay.

C: Please don't make me feel bad about this. If I could tell you I would, but I can't.

C: It's just that there's this person and they need my attention right now.

D: I'm not trying to make you feel bad. I would never do that.

D: Person?

D: Can I call you tonight?

D: Cora?

# Chapter 22

From now until I ascend,
I promise to operate with honesty and integrity.

Three gentle pats between her shoulder blades ripped Cora out of her dream. She was standing in the grass field again, every blade overgrown and swaying in the wind.

"Cora, it's time to wake up."

The voice sounded like her dad. She was almost sleepy enough to let herself believe it. "No. I stay here."

"No. You go to school."

Cora huffed and spun like a crocodile, rolling herself up tighter in her blanket. "You're not my dad." Even with half her brain dreaming and the other half refusing to be conscious, she realized, almost immediately, that she'd said something wrong. The words prickled inside of her like cactus spines. She flipped over, peeling the cover back. "I didn't mean that the way it sounded."

Her (bald) uncle, who sat on the edge of her bed, smiled. "I know."

"I meant it literally. Not like in a bad way. Sorry. Thank you for letting me live here."

His eyebrows shot up in surprise. "What are you talking about? This is your home, too."

"Yeah." She yawned. "For now."

"For always. You're a Seville. This hotel is *ours*. Hmm." He clasped his hands together. "Did you know I used to work for the Oracle Council too?"

Cora's face automatically folded into an unhappy frown. The council could *go* somewhere for all she cared—forever and never come back. She never asked to be separated from her parents. She never asked to take her Flyer exam early. She never asked for a Challenge in the First. She never asked for them to make her new friends her Kindlings. She never asked to be this miserable.

And they never asked her what she wanted.

Cora sat up, rubbing her eyes and shaking her head simultaneously. She stayed up way too late celebrating Rose's successful Singe with everyone and then talking to Dylan. She passed out with her phone lying flat on her face. Hopefully, he didn't record her snoring.

"When your grandpa, my dad, died, we knew one of us would have to come here to take over the family business.

By the time we were born, Hotel Coeur had already been in our family for four generations. This used to be your dad's room."

"Really?" She looked around her still sparsely decorated room. Nothing in here felt like him. Except for her uncle, but that didn't count.

"Yeah. Ray volunteered to run Hotel Coeur because *of course* he did." He kind of rolled his eyes, which made Cora giggle. "He was older, it was his responsibility, he was better at matchmaking—he had a million reasons why it should be him. I agreed. I decided to go with him and help out for the first week or two because that's *my* responsibility. I'm the younger brother. I'm his backup.

"We get here. Everything's going well. The staff were great, and we didn't have to make any changes. I was working the front desk when this woman walked in. She interviewed for a job at a law firm and decided to stay in town for a few days. If she was going to be moving there for work, she wanted to get a feel for the city. She was also a Matchmaker and had heard 'good things' about the Seville twins."

"Aunt Tanya?" Cora asked.

He nodded. "I took one look at her and told Ray he could leave because I knew I was staying. There wasn't anything he could do to change my mind about it. We told the council, and they sent him off to Georgia, where he met your mom a week later."

"Do you know that story too?" she asked hopefully. Her parents never told her how they met.

"Not enough details to make it good, but that's not why I told you mine," he said. "We don't know why, but everything always happens in tandem for us. Something important happens to him, and then the same thing will happen to me. Give or take a couple of days. Meeting Tanya was the first time I went first. Rose being born was the second—I became a dad first. That was when I realized not only was the tandem thing strange but that I had always been behind him. And then we all noticed the same thing was happening to you and Rose. Everything that happens to her happens to you shortly after."

Cora crumbled. "Are you saying we have a family curse? Because I don't think I can handle knowing that right now."

"No, we don't think it's a curse." He laughed. "It's something that's a part of who we are now, as a family. Rose is my baby girl, but when I look at you? I see me. Always running after my brother, trying to catch up, never feeling like I'm good enough. It took me a long time to realize that actually, I am." He tapped her nose. "Thankfully, I think you're moving a lot faster than I did. Anyway, all that to say, we"—he pointed between them—"are the same. You are *my* family. As long as I belong here, so do you."

Cora smiled. "Thank you. I really think I needed that." She climbed out of her blanket cocoon and gave him a big hug. "Can I stay home from school?"

"Half day is the best I can do, and that's only because Jackie and Rose already left. I'll make you breakfast and drop you off." He stood up. "You know it's really hard to wake you up. I can see why Rose always puts her cold feet on you."

Cora arrived at school right at the start of lunch. The School Engagement Committee met together pretty much every day as they got closer to the dance. Nothing ever became too difficult. Partly because it was fully funded by the school. All the ticket sales from previous events went into a general fund, which the school matched, dollar for dollar. They had a really great budget to work with.

After they came up with the idea, she and Dylan mostly spent their time polishing the script, approving the other subcommittees' ideas, and helping when needed. However, they'd have to hold auditions for the teachers and chaperones who wanted to participate in a few days. Dylan really hoped to find the perfect killer who could fool everyone. Cora thought Mrs. Bond would be good in the role, but she didn't want to do it.

"Are you still having migraines?" Dylan asked as he walked her to class.

Cora said, "No. Why?"

"Oh. I thought you might since you're always wearing sunglasses now. Your teachers don't ask you to take them off?"

"No." She grinned. "Because I tell *them* I have migraines. My uncle even wrote me a note—the whole family is in on it."

"Is everything okay?"

She decided to give him an honest answer, even though she didn't have any. "Everyone says it will be."

"But you don't think so."

"I don't know." She shrugged. "I have to do something important, but I'm not sure if I really want to."

"Maybe I can help? You don't have to tell me what it is. Just tell me what I have to do. I trust you."

Cora considered his offer and wondered if there was a way to accept it without getting in trouble. After all, it was his match—shouldn't he have some say in it? "Do you know Ariel Meyer?"

"The name is familiar. Who's that?"

"This girl I met the other day. She's nice."

"Okay."

"I"—she paused, biting her lip—"I think you should meet her."

"Um, okay. When?"

"I don't know yet," Cora said, quickly changing her mind. Her classroom was up ahead. "I'll talk to you later."

"Cora, wait—"

"Later, okay?" She hurried inside her class.

This time when Cora left a message for her mom, she called back in less than an hour.

"Hi, Mom." She was sitting in the courtyard under the willow tree.

"Hi, how are you?"

"Not great," Cora admitted. "I was hoping you could give me some information."

"Is it about your challenge?"

"No, not exactly." She switched the phone to her other ear. "I know you can't help me. I'm not asking for that. Not exactly."

"Hmm." Her mom was silent for a moment. "Why don't we do this: you ask your questions, and if I can answer, I will. If I suspect it's about your challenge, I'll have to report the inquiry. Sound fair?"

Sometimes, Cora wished her mom could just be *her mom* and not Iesha Seville, Career Matchmaker Extraordinaire. "No, but I'll take it."

Her mom chuckled softly. "Then ask away."

"This person told me that it's not technically against the

rules to test our heartstrings with our Kindlings. Is that true?"

"I see." Even in those two words, Cora recognized her mom's curt, controlled tone: she was ticked off. Not quite mad, but well on her way. "What *else* did this *person* tell you?"

"They said sometimes the Oracle Council makes mistakes on purpose and they'll make matches that benefit them."

"Okay," her mom said, speaking slowly. "Cora, I don't want you to say anything else. I don't want you to give me any more specifics than you already have. I want you to listen to me."

A chill rippled down Cora's spine, and it had nothing to do with the blustery SF wind. "All right."

"When a Matchmaker creates a Connection with a Kindling, that bond is a sacred act of trust. In most cases, we don't have to do anything to earn that trust. They sense our noble intentions and let us in. They tell us their secrets; we can predict and influence their moods; we can literally see what they want most in the world.

"You could also say it gives the Matchmaker power over their Kindling. A Connection automatically creates a power imbalance. We know too much, we have too much power, and the Connection *will* blur the lines of consent during a Singe. That is why Matchmakers must never, ever match themselves with their Kindlings. It is forbidden in every sense of the word.

"Now, if the purpose of testing heartstring compatibility is all in service of facilitating a match, do you understand why it's a bad idea for a Matchmaker to throw themselves into the mix? While testing is *technically* not against the rules, doing so will not result in anything productive or safe. Sometimes simply knowing is too much temptation."

Cora let the words sink in. She knew all of that, but not in the context of a Matchmaker selfishly putting themselves first. Because that was what it boiled down to, wasn't it?

Rose was willing to risk completely failing her challenge to perform a risky instant-Singe for Samantha and Ryan. If they turned into enemies-to-lovers, their ending was in the name. Eventually they would be together because a match was a match. Rose would have failed her challenge, but she would have done right by her Kindling in the long run.

*You're too cerebral.*

*No,* she decided. She might be that too, but her main problem was she was selfish. Rose was right—Cora hadn't thought about Samantha at all when she convinced Rose to walk away.

Cora didn't want to be the kind of Matchmaker who would choose to put her own happiness above Dylan's and Ariel's. This was their time. This was her duty. And as his friend, she owed him nothing but the very best she was capable of.

She nodded as if her mom could see it. "I understand," she said quietly, holding on to the front of her shirt.

"I have to go," her mom said. "We'll talk about this again once your challenge is over, okay? I know you'll do the right thing."

ARIEL: Banshee.

A: Changeling.

A: Mermaid.

A: Selkie.

A: My dad wants to know if you'll come over for dinner again.
   He likes your jokes.

CORA: Sure.

A: Were-llama.

A: Sasquatch.

A: Sassenach.

C: I wish.

A: Do you like movies?

C: Sure.

A: Want to have a movie night at my house after dinner?

C: Sure.

A: Sure is beginning to sound less and less positive here.

C: Sure :) ?

A: Much better.

A: Cherub.

A: Cupid.

C: No.

A: ???

# Chapter 23

Blue Letters arrived in a plume of smoke.

This one showed up right after Rose finished working in the café with Samantha at the crack of dawn. She was only allowed to do it once a week, for no pay, but hanging out and slightly annoying Samantha made it worth it.

Rose was in her treasured middle elevator, going back up to the penthouse, when a strange sound echoed around her before culminating in an audible *whomp*. She accidentally inhaled some of the smoke—it tasted and smelled like a beach fire left to smolder for too long. Gross. Coughing and waving her hand in front of her face, she picked the Blue Letter up off the ground.

> Attn: Roseanna Seville
>
> Re: Test Results from Challenge in the First

Well, in that case.

She tore into the envelope to read the card inside.

On this day, it is hereby acknowledged that ROSEANNA SEVILLE has passed the endeavor known as "Challenge in the First" courtesy of the Oracle Council with a score of ninety-two out of a possible one hundred points, well within the acceptable range.

Ten points were deducted for guardian manipulation.

Two points were awarded for the successful execution of an instant-Singe; an advanced spell well above her skill level.

Man, Christine was right about the grading scale being a scam.

ROSEANNA SEVILLE has also been awarded a necklace with a winged pendant to denote her new temporary rank of Flapper. The change in title does not come with any additional benefits or bonuses.

Rose snorted with laughter. "Who came up with that name?" She put the necklace on before shoving the folded envelope and card into her back pocket. The last thing she needed was for her family to make a fuss over it.

The day was about Cora and Cora only.

Inside their suite, her mom sat on the couch with her laptop propped up on a stack of books. "Oh, honey, come here, please. Someone wants to say hi." She stood up, ready to trade places. "I'm going to check on Cora. I'll be right back."

Rose was quick, but the power of her manners was thankfully quicker. Instead of grimacing like she wanted to, she put her Princess Perfect smile on.

"Oh, hi, Mrs. Swift." Her voice wavered—and her mom shot her a warning glance as she entered Cora's room. "How are you?"

"I'm doing good." Last time Rose saw her, Mrs. Swift had super straight, blond hair that reached her waist. It pretty much looked the same on-screen, framing her pinkish-toned face like a sharply pressed curtain. She also had three nose piercings and a flower tattoo on her neck. "Congratulations on passing your challenge. Your mom was just telling me how difficult it was."

"Yeah. It was."

"When we hadn't heard news, we started to get worried. Julien finished his in just under seventy-two hours, you know," she bragged, adding a knowing look. Rose's dad called Mrs. Swift a stage mom. It was possible to be famous in the matchmaking world. Her family was for many reasons, but someone's best bet was to do something notable and worth talking about. For parents, that usually meant having gifted kids.

Rose kept it together. "I do now."

"Oh, he'll probably want to say hi." She looked behind her and called out, "Julien? Could you come here, please?"

"You don't have to do that. You *really* don't," Rose said, even though she knew there was no point. Their moms *always* forced them to interact with each other.

"Just one second." She got up and walked out of frame.

Maybe if Rose hit the disconnect button fast enough, she could blame it on a bad connection. Right as she leaned forward, Julien sat down.

The sunlight hit the window exactly right, bathing his pale, freckled skin in a soft afternoon glow. He'd be cute if he weren't so insufferably annoying, with his curly black hair that was actually, *apparently*, a dark brown. He corrected her enough times about it for her to remember. The winged Flapper pendant rested right in the V created by his button-up shirt.

"Rose." He tugged on his collar, looking uncomfortable.

"Swift."

"What happened to nemesis?"

"Do you *want* me to call you that?"

"No. Julien would be nice, but I guess my last name is fine."

Julien was the last person she wanted to see, but she

decided that nemeses might not be a good thing to have. Look at how wrong she'd been about Samantha—maybe the same was true for him.

All her memories of him felt so vivid, as if they were in motion. There was never a time in her life when he wasn't present, getting on her nerves and competing with her. Which was funny because she didn't remember ever meeting him for the first time. Something was there in place of where a memory should be—a giant white spot as if someone had taken paint and covered it up.

He said, "Congrats, I guess."

"Same to you." They sat there in awkward silence for precisely ten seconds before Rose asked, "What did they make you do?"

"What?"

"The council. What was your challenge like?"

"It was pretty standard. Two Kindlings, seventy-two hours, long distance. I got a ninety-seven."

Rose raised an eyebrow. "I see." His mom conveniently left that part out. He finished so fast because he had to.

Julien cleared his throat. "I heard they gave you a hard time."

"Oh, I wouldn't call a magic-resistant solo-Kindling with a two-week time limit *hard*."

His jaw dropped. "You're lying."

"And why would I do that? I'm very proud of my

ninety-two, thank you very much."

"How did you— What? How? How did you even pull that off?"

"An instant-Singe."

He blinked in surprise. "No."

"Yeah. But I'm glad you had a good old standard time."

"Rose, that's really impressive. I'm not even kidding. Did you really?"

Taken aback by his excited tone, she held the contents of her Blue Letter up to the camera and pointed to it.

"No way. How did you do it? Weren't you scared it would backfire?"

"Strangely, no. I was scared about a lot of other things, but not that. I just really believed in the match. I knew I was right."

He whistled. *"Wow."*

"Yeah." She nodded. "Anyway, I should go. I have to get ready for Cora's dance."

"I heard she got a challenge too." He looked skeptical. "How'd she do?"

And just like that, all the goodwill he'd earned with Rose vanished. Poof. Gone. He might not be her nemesis anymore, but she still didn't like him. It seemed some people were destined to be insufferable forever.

"She planned it for tonight. We'll know soon, but I'm not worried." Rose shook her head. "And by the way, did you *also* hear the council confirmed she's a diviner with *two* abilities?"

"*What?*"

"Oh, look at the time! Gotta go! Bye!" She closed the laptop lid. It was way more satisfying to hang up on him that way.

Rose stood up and headed to Cora's room. Surviving an infinity week (the kind where it's both impossibly long and incredibly short) took a certain kind of daring. But Cora had made it. Their masquerade ball dresses were hung on the back of the door, shoes not far away in their boxes.

What sucked the most was there wasn't really anything Rose could do to help Cora. She had to watch, helpless, as she began withdrawing into herself. Cora told fewer jokes, smiled less often, and her missing laughter haunted Rose as much as her defeated, sad eyes.

"Ready to get ready?" she asked.

"As ready as I'll ever be." Cora looked up from her phone, fake smile stapled in place.

Chapter

24

From now until I ascend,
I promise to follow my Kindlings' hearts.

Cora chose a pastel rainbow for a dress.
It was sleeveless with a tight knotted bodice, and a floor-length skirt that made her feel like a Greek goddess walking. She twirled in the mirror feeling genuinely happy for the first time in days. She had piled her hair up into a high ponytail, braided it in singles, and then wound the braids into a giant bun. Lastly, she decorated it with star bobby pins, creating constellations.

"Makeup?" Cora asked hopefully.

"Your mom says no," Aunt Tanya said sweetly, and tapped Cora's nose.

"I'd just sweat it off dancing anyway." She managed not to pout. Rose had been allowed to wear makeup for two years already.

"You look beautiful without it."

"That's not the point," she said. "I want to be even more beautiful by expressing my creativity on my face."

"Is that the lie makeup companies are selling these days?"

"It's not a lie. Well, maybe it is a little." She laughed.

"Dad's ready to go." Rose popped her head (and makeup-having face) in the doorway. Her dress was a beautiful maroon color, and she wore a silver-and-gold cape they found at a costume store. "Stop being so beautiful. Oh my god, I want people to look at me too, you know."

Cora felt Rose's emotions tugging at her. They wanted her to see, begging her to understand. She concentrated on pushing them gently away. *Not today. Please.* She had her own problems to deal with. Taking on more might break her. She said quietly, "I'm not telling you how you feel, but I know you're feeling."

"Sorry," Rose whispered back, dropping the act. "I'll keep it down over here so you can focus tonight."

"Thank you." She gave her cousin the best hug she could manage. "We can cry together later."

"I already got my sunglasses picked out."

Uncle Norman dropped them off directly in front of the venue. A line had begun to form with everyone wearing masks and capes, carrying gloves and canes and hand fans. The dance would be a success. Everyone was going to love it and at least one thing was guaranteed to go right that night. Cora and Rose bypassed the line heading for the doors. All the committee members and their guests were supposed to meet inside for a quick meeting before the event started.

In an office, off to the side of the main ballroom, Cora found Dylan waiting with who had to be Jax and Jill.

"Skittles!" Jax exclaimed.

"Eh?" Cora asked.

"You're a rainbow!"

"Oh—oh no. Bad joke. Bad," Cora said.

"You look great," Dylan said to her.

"So do you." They had color coordinated. He went with a classic charcoal-gray suit and pastel rainbow tie.

"For you." He handed her a mint-colored rose corsage.

"Aren't these for prom?"

"I say they're for whenever I want to give you flowers at a dance."

"Can't argue with that." She looked into his eyes and said, "I love it."

"It's nice to finally meet you, Cora. He"—Jill nodded to Dylan—"talks about you a lot. Some would say too much, maybe." Her smile was just as beautiful as her royal-blue dress that stopped at the knees and had sheer lace sleeves.

Mrs. Bond entered the office and began the meeting. Her 1950s-inspired red dress and hairdo made her look like a model straight out of a vintage catalog. They reviewed the full agenda and ensured everyone knew their marks, their lines, and had all their assigned props hidden under their clothes.

Once the doorman was in position, the front doors opened and everyone began to file in.

"Whoa," Jax said. "What kind of budget did you have for this thing?"

The decoration committee had really outdone themselves bringing Dylan's vision to life. Entering the transformed ballroom felt like moving through a diamond kaleidoscope. The unreal effect had been added to the walls, parts of the floor, and the tables and chairs. As they walked inside, they were each handed a transparent LED balloon at the door. The dance floor was filled with them. If Cora squinted, all she could see were bouncing lights, which reflected off the diamond illusion and it was . . . incredible. She'd never seen anything like it.

If this had to be her last date with Dylan, at least it would be somewhere magnificent.

"Should we get a table or hit the dance floor first?" Dylan asked.

"Dance. Definitely." She tugged him forward.

The entertainment committee picked a perfect DJ too. They played a great mix of different genres and styles, all the songs seamlessly blending from one to the next. Songs they could shout the chorus to. Deep cuts that almost no one knew but were so infectious by the end they'd want to hear it again and again. Power ballads they slow danced to and sang with feeling. Every inch of the space pulsed with feel-good energy. If someone was sitting, they were nodding their head and moving their shoulders. If they were walking, they moved in time to the beat. It would have been impossible to not want to dance.

Cora and Dylan danced in a disjointed circle with their friends, keeping close together. He moved exactly how she pictured he would—smooth and fluid, using his limbs in perfect sync with hips and footwork. Part of her wanted to stop and just watch him. She wanted to memorize the entire moment and lock it away for safekeeping.

When the opening chords of a slow song began, he took an automatic step toward Cora. Her arms around his neck. His hands at her hips. Pressed in close. She could feel him breathing, feel his heart beating next to hers.

"You're so beautiful," he whispered in her ear.

The difference from what he had said earlier—"you look" to "you are"—hit her hard. Each word unintentionally cut into her. She raised her eyes to the ceiling to keep from crying.

It wouldn't be much longer now.

★ ★ ★

Cora had planned her Singe down to the minute.

The masquerade murder mystery would officially start at 9:00 p.m.

She and Ariel agreed to meet by the drinks table at 8:45 p.m. When Cora spotted her, she'd tell Dylan there was someone she wanted him to meet. She'd introduce them, use the Conduit, and . . . that would be that.

"Want to get some air?" Dylan asked, pointing to the doors that led to the outer patio area.

They had found a table after deciding they needed a break from dancing.

"I'm okay. Let's just stay," she said, trying to keep cool.

"You sure?"

"Yeah! I'm okay." She smiled at him to prove her point. Big and bright as she could make it.

Dylan nodded and began chewing on his bottom lip. He leaned in close again. "Maybe—maybe we could just go for a few minutes?"

"Are *you* okay?" she asked, instantly worried. He'd seemed fine so far. They were dancing! And laughing! Everything had been, in a word, perfect.

"Yeah. I'm okay." He gave her an easy smile. "I just want to talk to you."

"We're talking now."

"Talk somewhere quieter."

Cora couldn't help it—she looked at the drinks table. Still no Ariel.

"It's kind of important," he whispered near her ear again and pulled back so she could see his face.

"Important?"

He nodded. "Please?"

Someday, Cora might be able to say no to his face. That day was not right then. He took her hand and led her outside. She made sure they stood at a decent angle to keep the drinks table in her sights.

"Much better," he said.

It was a little cold. She hunched her shoulders near her ears to keep warm.

"Oh, do you want my jacket?" He started taking it off.

She held up her hand. "No, I'm fine. Thank you. So, what did you want to talk about?"

"Well," he said slowly. "I've been thinking. And I was wondering if—what are you looking at?"

"What?" Cora focused on him instead of the table. "Nothing. Sorry. Go ahead."

"Are you sure you're okay? You seem kind of tense."

"Do I? No. No, I'm not tense."

Tense? Not really. Nervous? *Absolutely.* She was nearly out of her mind with nerves. She'd bypassed pins and needles and jumped straight to juggling steak knives.

Dylan playfully narrowed his eyes. "You're still not going to tell me what's going on, are you?"

"Nope." No point in lying.

"Then can I have two minutes?" he asked. "Two minutes of your undivided attention."

"Two minutes," she repeated, still focused on the table. "Okay. Two minutes."

Cora took one look at his face—soft and cute and vulnerable—and she wanted to *die*. She wanted to drop dead on the spot because this was not happening to her. Not here, not now. *NO*.

"I know we haven't known each other that long," Dylan began, "and I know how this is going to sound, but I'm going to say it anyway. I really like you, Cora. More than I think I've ever liked anyone. Ever. You're my favorite person. You're my favorite *everything*. I think about you all the time. I go to bed and you're in my head. I wake up and you're in my head. It's just all Cora, all the time."

She couldn't move. Her chest rose and fell in exaggerated movements, a hairbreadth away from hyperventilation.

"I'm not sure what any of that means other than I like you. I like talking to you and spending time with you. And I just wanted you to know that." He paused and the small laugh that escaped turned into a smile. "I'm not asking anything or for anything, you know? I just had this weird dream about you disappearing. I woke up really freaked out and I thought, *You have to tell her before it's too late.*"

"Disappearing?" It was the only word she could manage.

"Yeah. Everything was the same except I started seeing less and less of you. Like you were fading away from me. *Just* me. Everyone else could still see you, but I couldn't."

Cora nodded. "I don't think I'm going anywhere," she said softly. "I hope I'm not."

"Good. Because I don't want you to."

She nodded again, reaching for a smile and finding one just for him. "There's someone special I want you to meet."

Ariel had spotted her and was already walking toward them. Cora waited by the door with Dylan at her side, still holding hands. There wasn't any point in meeting her halfway. She wore a white jumpsuit with a gold belt tied around her waist. A white flower had been placed above her left ear.

"Hey," Ariel said. "You said soda table at eight forty-five."

"I did."

"And you weren't there."

"I wasn't."

"For shame."

"You better believe it."

Ariel laughed. "Love the dress by the way."

"Thank you. It required a lot of undignified begging to convince my parents to buy it for me," Cora said. "Anyway, Ariel this is Dylan. Dylan this is my friend Ariel."

Quietly, Cora grabbed hold of Ariel's wrist.

A Matchmaker could truly create a Conduit out of anything. The best ones ended up being something the Kindlings had in common. Initially, Cora planned to use a camera, since they both loved photography, but then she realized there was something else. Something bigger and more powerful.

Her.

Concentrating with all her might, Cora allowed herself to become the Conduit that connected her new friends' hearts together.

DYLAN: Where did you go?

CORA: Family emergency. I'm sorry.

C: Please keep Ariel company for me? I promised I'd stay with her.

D: She's okay. She's helping us pack up.

D: Are you okay?

C: I miss you.

# Epilogue

It felt deeply ironic that Dylan's match was named Ariel because Cora felt like the original little mermaid. The one Hans Christian Andersen forced to suffer for the entire story. Cora had made the same choice—to willingly give her prince to someone else.

Cora remembered the spectacular sight and all-encompassing feel of their Connection before it was destroyed by the Singe. It was real. It had been everything. And in a way, it would continue to be. Before she forced herself to go home, as if he could hear her thoughts, Dylan caught her eye from across the room. He smiled at her while he slow danced with Ariel. His nose crinkled as he did it, slightly embarrassed but happy and okay with showing it. A private moment he shared with Cora and Cora alone.

Because a bond like theirs, new as it was, could never be burned away.

Cora slipped her sunglasses back on and left her room. She heard voices in the kitchen, so she followed them—she didn't feel like being alone anymore and was thirsty anyway.

Rose spotted her first. "Hey, hey, you're up!"

"Yeah. Need water." She walked to the fridge. Unable to wait, she cracked the bottle open, downing a fourth of it in almost a single gulp.

"Uhhh, Cora?" Rose asked in a strange voice.

"What?" She looked at her cousin standing next to her uncle . . . who suddenly had hair.

Why did Uncle Norman have hair? Cora frowned— and then dropped the bottle of water. "Dad?"

"Don't tell me you forgot how to tell us apart?" Her dad laughed.

Cora didn't remember rocket launching herself across the room, but she must have because he picked her up in a giant bear hug. She buried her face in his fluffy sweater—it smelled kind of gross, like stale airplane air and pretzels, but she didn't care.

When he put her down, her mom was there too. "Sunglasses?" she asked, pulling her into a hug.

"Necessary evil," Cora said, crying her eyes out again, for the millionth time that week. "My eyes decided they wanted to turn into a magical puffer fish."

"Oh," Cora's mom said, holding her tighter. She was almost everything Cora hoped to be when she grew up. They already looked alike with the same brown-colored skin and big dark brown eyes, so she felt like she was halfway there. However, her mom was tall enough to tower over most people and confident enough to wear high heels anyway. She didn't know how to do casual, instead getting dressed every day as if she were about to head to her office complete with makeup and hair, which she had just changed to a fantastic chin-length bob. "Oh, my baby. I know how hard tonight was. I'm so immensely proud of you."

Her dad placed a hand on the top of her head. "We tried to make it for your masquerade ball, but our flight got delayed. We're proud of you for being vice chair," he said. "We're proud of you for everything you do."

"Who wants pancakes?" Rose asked, jumping up and down. "Because I do. Let's get pancakes at that twenty-four-hour diner that's not too far from here."

"I'll place an order for pickup," her uncle said, already using his phone.

Twenty minutes later, Cora's entire family sat around the dining room table, having breakfast for almost-midnight dinner. All under one roof. She sat between her parents, feeling so happy her face hurt from smiling so much. She could barely eat the pancakes, which were bigger than her head, because her dad kept making her laugh.

And then in an unexpected puff of smoke, two envelopes appeared in the center of the table. A Blue Letter that read:

Attn: Coretta Marjorie Seville

Re: Test Results from Challenge in the First

And a Green Letter that read:

Attn: The Seville Family of Hotel Coeur

Cora picked up her envelope, opened it straightaway, and read it aloud.

On this day, it is hereby acknowledged that CORETTA MARJORIE SEVILLE has passed the endeavor known as "Challenge in the First" courtesy of the Oracle Council with a perfect score of one hundred out of a possible one hundred points, exceeding all expectations.

CORETTA MARJORIE SEVILLE has also been awarded a necklace with a winged pendant to denote her new temporary rank of Flapper. The change in title does not come with any additional benefits or bonuses.

"There's a necklace for you inside." Rose held up the one she was already wearing. "See?"

Cora turned the envelope upside down. The necklace slid into her palm. Hers was slightly different from Rose's—a small green stone was embedded in the center.

"Not bad for a late bloomer."

Both of her parents kissed her forehead. "We're so proud of you."

She wasn't sure how she felt about her score, her new title, or necklace. They were good things—things to be proud of. But she didn't understand why she had to go through so much to deserve them.

"What about the other envelope?" Rose asked.

None of the adults moved to pick it up.

Aunt Tanya sighed. "Well, someone open it."

"*What is it?*" Cora and Rose asked together.

"I'll do it." Cora's mom grabbed it with a frown. "Green letters can be a summons or an invitation. This one is"—she paused to read the letter—"they want to do a facility check. They're inviting Hotel Coeur to be one of the three West Coast camp locations this year."

"Oh. My. God." Rose began bouncing in her seat.

Once a year, all the Matchmakers ages ten to nineteen were required to attend a formal training camp for two weeks. The Oracle Council hosted different locations worldwide that they got to choose from. Rose went to Canada her first year and the Philippines her second. Both times, Cora went to Iceland because her parents had been assigned to work the camp there.

"No, we are *not* doing that here," Uncle Raymond insisted. "No. The answer's no."

Cora and Rose exchanged a look. If they learned anything from the past few weeks, it was that the Oracle Council would do exactly what they wanted.

Auntie Jackie was right.

After dinner, Cora dragged herself to the shower and brushed her teeth before diving into her bed.

She did it. Everything worked out. She survived her first challenge and heartbreak.

Because that definitely happened. Auntie Jackie even read her heartstrings to make sure.

It still hurt. It might always hurt. She pressed a hand to her chest—she was alone. The power of a Singe had burned their Connection away. She'd never be able to reach Dylan like that again.

Her phone began to vibrate on the bedside table.

Cora laughed. How long would her heart continue to leap at the sight of his name. "Hello?"

"Hey," Dylan said. "Are you sleeping?"

"On my way," she said, snuggling her pillows. "Did Ariel make it home okay?"

"Yeah. I waited with her until her dad picked her up," he said. "It's so weird. I've seen her around before at school, but I never talked to her until tonight. She's, uh, nice."

Ah, there it was. She heard it in his voice—the beginnings of a soft longing that would only grow with time.

Singes didn't automatically make Kindlings fall head over heels in love with their match forever and ever. It could happen, of course, but usually the aftermath took a slower, more deliberate route.

A Matchmaker placed them on the path. The rest was up to them.

"Yeah, she is," she agreed.

He cleared his throat. "So, is everything okay with you? You kind of Cinderella'd me."

"I did not. I left way before midnight with both of my shoes," she joked. "My parents came home."

"For real?"

"Yeah." She laughed, feeling genuinely giddy. "They flew home to surprise me."

"Oh, that's amazing. I'm so happy for you." His tone turned serious as he said, "I was worried you left because of what I said."

"What do you mean?" She heard the sound of rustling sheets. "You're home too, right?"

"Yeah. I've been here for a bit. Getting ready to go to sleep, so I had to do my nightly ritual of calling. I'm very predictable like that."

"It's okay. I don't mind," she said sleepily, pushing aside the fact that their calls were probably numbered. She wanted to collect this moment too, even though he'd want to start calling Ariel instead soon.

"About what I said earlier—"

"That's okay too. Don't worry about it."

"I'm not worried about it." He laughed nervously. "I just wanted to make sure that you knew that I meant it. Every word."

"I know."

"And I thought maybe I scared you off. I really wasn't asking for anything, I promise."

"I'm not scared. Don't be weird," she said quietly. "I feel the same way."

"Don't disappear, okay?" he whispered. "Stay with me."

Cora smiled, eyes closing as she fell asleep. "I'll be here as long as you want."

# Glossary

**Career Matchmakers:** Matchmakers who are employed by the Oracle Council. One may not apply for a position; they are exclusively available by invitation only.

**Compatibility:** An evaluation of heartstrings, interests, and all other factors a Matchmaker deems relevant when facilitating a match between Kindlings. Alternatively, it is also used when selecting the best match for solo-Kindlings.

**Conduit:** A bespelled object of utmost importance during a Singe. When in use, it will connect the heartstrings of a Kindling(s) to the object of their desire, allowing them to safely open their heart to new possibilities.

**Connection:** A powerful, psychic bond designed to link a Matchmaker to their Kindlings.

**Diviner:** A Matchmaker with the rare innate ability of divination. Manifestation may vary, but will involve some form of seeing the unseen.

**Generations:** A generation is defined by all the Matchmakers born within a given year.

**Guidebook:** An indispensable magical tool given to Fledglings to aid in their Matchmaker training.

**Heart-shaped mole:** Every Matchmaker develops this rather quirky beauty mark upon gaining access to their channel. It can appear anywhere on their body.

**Heartstrings:** A physical manifestation of the desire(s) residing deep within a human heart. They vary in color, size, and shape.

**Instant-Singe:** A formidable spell designed to create a magical bridge between two hearts, regardless of compatibility. While highly effective, it has an abysmal success rate and is not recommended. The use of this spell is monitored by the Oracle Council. They have been known to issue fines and/or penalties for failed attempts.

**Kindling:** Any human assigned to a Matchmaker by the Oracle Council. More often than not, they are assigned in predetermined pairs.

**Late Bloomer:** Refers to younglings who belong to a Matchmaking family but did not exhibit a channeling ability by their fifth birthday, per the standard.

**Leeching:** Refers to the unauthorized theft of Singe energy. It is explicitly forbidden for a Matchmaker to steal a fellow Matchmaker's magic.

**Matchmaker Hierarchy:** There are three primary age classifications: Fledgling (Years 5–12), Flyer (Years 13–19), and Matchmaker–in–arms (adults).

**Red Letter:** The method the Oracle Council uses to notify Matchmakers of their assigned Kindlings.

**Whirlwind Matchmakers:** A specialized field of match-making, pioneered by Jacqueline Evette Ross in her twenty-second year and officially recognized by the Oracle Council shortly thereafter.

**Wunderkind:** A title bestowed upon the most exemplary Matchmakers in any given generation. The current Fledgling Wunderkinds of Year 12 are Miss Rose Seville and Mr. Julien Swift.

# Acknowledgments

So far, every book that I've published has been a wild ride from start to finish. *Harmony and Heartbreak* is no exception. In 2014, I had an idea for a book about a young matchmaking fairy. I wrote a full manuscript, truly loved it with my whole heart, but no one wanted to represent or publish that book. And then, seemingly out of nowhere a whole six years later, an opportunity to write about a pair of matchmaking cousins crossed my path.

Sometimes good things really do come to those who wait.

A million and one thank-yous to:

Claudia Gabel and Sophie Schmidt for their fantastic edit letters and brainstorming sessions, Lissy Marlin for creating the wonderful cover art, and the entire team at HarperCollins who helped make *Harmony and Heartbreak* into a real book.

My agent, Carrie Pestritto.

My Usual Suspects: my family, SHINee, Sarah, and Anna. And also my very vocal cat, Bebe, who won't stop yelling for attention as I type this sentence.

Makers of the amazing pop music that kept twelve-year-old me alive and inspired much-older me while drafting this book.

Slim's in San Francisco: You've closed your doors forever but you'll always have a special place in my heart (and in my books!).

And as always, thank you for taking the time to read a piece of my heart.

See you in the next one,

Claire ♡